SONG OF LAUGHTER

LAURAINE SNELLING

THORNDIKE PRESS

An imprint of Thomson Gale, a part of The Thomson Corporation

Detroit • New York • San Francisco • New Haven, Conn. • Waterville, Maine • London

LIBRARY OF CONGRESS CATALOGING-IN-PUBLICATION DATA

Snelling, Lauraine.
  Song of laughter / by Lauraine Snelling.
    p. cm. — (Thorndike Press large print Christian romance)
  ISBN-13: 978-1-4104-0427-5 (alk. paper)
  ISBN-10: 1-4104-0427-7 (alk. paper)
    1. Widows — Fiction. 2. Washington (State) — Fiction. 3. Large type books. I. Title.
  PS3569.N39S67 2008
  813'.54—dc22   2007041267

Published in 2008 by arrangement with Lauraine Snelling.

Printed in the United States of America on permanent paper
10 9 8 7 6 5 4 3 2 1

To Wayne, who loved the farm as much as I did. Thank you for encouraging me and supporting me so I can write.

With love and gratitude to Noreen Brownlie and Jerry Chan who gave of themselves, their home, and their time that this book could be finished in time for the Golden Heart Contest. Friends like these are the gifts God gives beyond measure.

Thanks also to the other members of our Portland critique group, Lynn Jordan, Beverly Fletcher, and before she moves, Annette Broadrick. When we're together again, it's like the years between have never been. That's the test of true friendship.

ONE

"Sorry, old girl —" Lareana stroked the old milk cow's velvety throat — "that's all for tonight." Then with a screech of metal on metal, the barred gate swung open and the bell cow of the Three Trees herd ambled out the door. Lareana pushed levers, closing one gate and opening another to admit the next candidate into the milking parlor. As the idea flitted through her mind, she smiled to herself. *"Other ladies dress in their finest and entertain guests in their parlors, but look at me!"* Giving her faded jeans a rueful look, she pushed back a few tendrils of honey-blond hair — "if this pit can be called a parlor, that is."

She paused a moment to survey her cramped quarters. The concrete enclosure where the dairy cows were simultaneously fed and hooked up to the milking machines more nearly resembled a deep stall. The cow on her left stopped munching long enough

7

to stare at her with baleful brown eyes, then returned to her feed bin.

Lareana stood at shoulder level with the cows' udders to slip into position the four suction cups connected to long tubes that would pipe the milk directly to the cooling tank. With a cow on either side of her, she was forced to be efficient in her movements, but she always took time for the petting and individual attention the herd had come to expect in the six long months since her husband John had died.

" 'Step into my parlor, said the lady to the cow'," she parodied an old nursery rhyme. When the animal glared at her for not cranking the feed handle immediately, Lareana's laughter was music floating like dust motes in a sunbeam. "You just don't appreciate good poetry, my girl. Don't you know —"

"Know what?"

Lareana whirled. A small shriek escaped her lips and her heart raced as all the blood drained from her face. "Who . . . who —" She took a deep breath and tried again. "Who are —"

"Hey, sorry!" called the tall stranger leaning against the door frame. "I didn't mean to frighten you."

"Well, then, you're just naturally good at

it!" Seeing that the man appeared genuinely remorseful, Lareana willed her stomach back below her tonsils. "I — I just didn't hear you come in."

"How could you?" His grin crinkled the corners of sky blue eyes. "You were too busy messing up that poem."

"Didn't like my version, huh?" Her mind flew ahead of her words, cataloguing the broad shoulders that stretched a plaid shirt, worn jeans, and scuffed boots. The leather gloves, carelessly clasped in one bronzed hand, clued her in. "You're the new hay hauler."

He nodded, emanating power leashed and at rest. With two fingers he tipped the brim of his sweat-darkened felt hat. "You got it."

"Where's Bud?"

"Down setting up the elevator." The man gestured toward the aging barn. "Sent me up to let someone know we're here."

"Uncle Haakan's gone for the evening. We didn't expect you until tomorrow." She turned to remove one of the machines. "I won't be done for —" she closed her eyes, calculating mentally — "for at least another hour."

"We'll manage." He smiled again and glanced down at the infant seat parked in the doorway. The device cradled a soundly sleeping four-month-old baby. "You always have an audience when you milk?"

"Yep. Johnny's my rooting section. The rhythm of the machines works better than a rocking chair."

An incoming cow bellowed, the sound ricocheting off the cement block walls. The tow-headed tot flinched, sucked once on the thumb in his mouth, and relaxed again.

"See?" Love turned her azure eyes to shimmering pools.

The man froze. Golden rays from the late sun slanted through the high windows, burnishing the slim figure before him. In the light, this rustic setting with mother and child was an artist's daydream. He blinked, then forced his mind back from the illusion.

The woman's smile again caressed the sleeping infant, then rose to warm the man's face also. She finished her sentence, "He likes it here."

"Can't say as I blame him, even with all this noise." The man grinned again as he turned to go, eying her appreciatively. "And by the way, I like your shirt." Whistling the opening bars of "Some Enchanted Evening," he closed the screen door softly behind him.

Lareana glanced down at the front of her navy sweatshirt. The words "Nuzzle My

Muzzle" arched above two red Duroc piglets, snout to snout. She chuckled, then caught herself humming along.

"Silly," she chided herself, "you didn't even ask him his name."

Having learned through experience that she could not hurry when milking cows, Lareana continued at her habitual pace. Her mind, however, refused to stay inside the milking parlor. It flitted to the man in the barn, to the dinner she had left simmering in the crockpot, and back to the recurring problems that nibbled like mice at the corners of her consciousness. How would she keep the farm operating at peak efficiency now that John was gone? Four hundred acres with 150 milking cows was . . . well, it was almost too much for *two strong men* to manage, let alone a woman and her elderly uncle. Besides, the income barely supported their two families.

To bring in some additional funds, she had considered increasing the herd, but she would have to sell that forty-acre piece of property out by the freeway first. And she needed to hire some more part-time help. She heaved a deep sigh. It seemed a Catch-22 situation. Selling out might still be the best option, after all.

Shrugging aside the negative thought, she

squared her shoulders. "We're going to make it," she vowed to the last cow to enter the stall. "I'm going to keep this farm. John and I worked too hard to give up now."

Little John had finished his nap and was well on his way to getting bored and fussy before Lareana gave the cow she was milking a sharp slap on the rump and sent her out the door.

"Almost done, Johnny," she crooned as she set him out of the way so she could hose down the milking parlor and holding pen, then run soapy water through the milk lines.

But soft promises were no longer sufficient, and his eyes were brimming with angry tears when she finally hoisted the infant seat onto one hip. Setting the automatic agitator for the huge stainless steel milk tank, her eye caught the date on the wall calendar — October 10. Only three more weeks before the drunk who had killed John would come to trial.

The baby in her arms kicked his feet and gurgled. Lareana unclenched her teeth and flipped the switch. "Your turn, son. You've been patient long enough." He accepted her apology with a toothless grin.

Outside, Lareana drew in a deep draught of the crisp October air. Dusk had deepened to dark, but the two mercury floodlights in the yard drove back the shadows as she walked swiftly up the graveled drive past the barn, noticing that the green semi-trailer was only half unloaded.

"Dinner will be ready when you are," she called to the man slinging hundred-pound bales of rich green alfalfa onto the electric elevator.

Bud's familiar weather-beaten face peered down from the stack of bales above her head, and he shouted over the elevator clicking and clanking the hay up to the loft. "Hi-yah, Lareana. My stomach says it's ready now, but it'll be another hour 'fore we're done here."

"That's okay. That'll give me time to feed my helper here and put him to bed." She nodded to the baby in her arms.

"Whatcha got there?" The burly man perched on a bale and squinted down. "Last time I saw you, you was big as a house. Thought you'd have triplets, for sure." He spat a brown stream of tobacco juice onto the floor.

"Thanks. You sure know how to make a woman feel good." Her chuckle was warm and throaty as she moved so he could see the baby.

"The name's Johnny, if that gives you a clue." As she turned, her eyes were drawn to the level gaze of the stranger in the loft.

"See you two later then?"

He nodded.

" 'You will see a stranger across a crowded room,' " Lareana serenaded baby Johnny as she headed for the square white house. Three ancient Douglas firs protected the two-story home from the north winds and dropped cones and needles on the pillared porch that flanked it on both sides.

Pausing in the front yard, she stopped for her evening commune with Mt. Rainier, the silver sentinel standing guard at the far end of the hay fields and the undulating fir-clad hills. "Thank You, God, for another day," she murmured, "for being like that mountain, for never leaving me — ever changing yet always the same." She hugged the infant seat close. Her eyes sought the stars, poking holes in the heavens above.

Down in a pasture, a cow lowed. The wistful sound was carried on the same breeze that stirred the branches above her and gently lifted the sun-kissed strands of her bangs. Lareana waited. The sense of peace deepened, wrapping itself around her like a giant hand, holding her safely in its grasp.

Stepping quietly, so as not to shatter the moment, Lareana swung open the gate, entered her mum-fenced yard, and clicked the gate shut behind her. Samson, her sable collie, was stretched out on the porch. He thumped his tail at her approach, then rose and looked toward the door expectantly.

"Where were you when the hay truck arrived?" At the sternness in her voice, his feathery tail drooped. "You're supposed to be guarding the place." His ears followed suit. He whimpered, dejection apparent in every line of his powerful body. "Off gallivanting, I'll bet. We should just call you Romeo." The dog dropped to the porch floor.

Lareana shook her head. "You sure can put on an act." She bent down to pet the drooping ears. "That must be some hussy down the road to make you miss the hay truck." The change in her voice worked a lightning-fast transformation in the dog. He sat up, his tongue lolling to one side of his mouth, then lifted one white paw and waited.

"Oh, all right, you're forgiven," she conceded, laughing and shaking the proffered paw. "I always have been a sucker for a male with nice manners."

Samson had his nose in the door almost before she had opened it. "Sit, boy. You forgot. Women and children first."

She entered, set the infant seat down on

the floor, and flicked on the light switch, bringing the delft blue and white kitchen to life. "All right, Samson. Come." He obeyed, wagging his tail with delight.

The aroma of home-baked beans wafted around her as she stepped outside once more to pull off her boots. She could hear Johnny gurgling and chattering at the dog who always sneaked in a quick lick when her back was turned.

From force of habit, she looked back toward the milk house, expecting to see John coming for dinner any minute. As the slowly dimming pain struck forcefully again, she remembered. John was dead. A loved one can be killed in an instant, but five-year-long habits of waiting and loving take longer to die.

She shut her eyes against the pain and tried to regain her sense of peace. Failing that, she muttered through clenched teeth, "I *will* praise the Lord. I *will*." Comfort stole around her shoulders, encircled her heart, and released the tension in her jaw.

The light streaming from her open door beckoned her back to the world of cooing infants and baking beans. But her sigh drifted toward the heavens, effectively communicating her deepest needs to the Father she trusted to listen.

Pink begonias blooming on the windowsill above the sink were reflected in the darkened window as Lareana washed her hands. She smiled at her reflection — "wholesome," her uncle always said — then brushed back tendrils of hair that insisted on a life of their own. Johnny, bored with pulling patient Samson's ears, whimpered.

"I'm coming, I'm coming," she promised the restless infant as she dried her hands. "Which do you want first, dinner or dry pants?" She lifted him from the seat, and the baby's questing mouth left no doubt about his choice. "Too bad, you're soaked."

Quickly, she changed him, then settled into the rocker in front of the wood stove. With one wool-stockinged toe, she twirled the handle on the door of the square black stove and opened it. The low-burning embers flamed briefly in the gust of air, and the warmth crept up her leg, bathed her face in its orange glow, and turned the collie at her feet into molten gold. It would be so easy to close her eyes and . . . a tiny fist rubbed against her chest. Baby John delivered a gargantuan belch, and his lashes fluttered softly into sleep.

Lareana gazed down at him, reluctant to let the moment go. During his four months of life, little John had grown to resemble his father more and more. The dimple in his chin matched the cleft in big John's, and the muddy gray of newborn eyes had deepened to the same cobalt blue. "Good night, darling." Then Lareana heard herself repeating the same words John had said to her every night just before they slept: "God loves you and so do I."

Carefully she eased herself and the sleeping baby from the chair. Johnny only sighed and popped a tiny thumb in his mouth as she tucked the blanket around him in his crib.

In her bedroom, Lareana dug a clean top out of the drawer and quickly donned it. On the way back to the kitchen, she stopped by the bathroom to run a brush through her hair and re-secure the leather clasp holding her ponytail in place. As an afterthought, she applied a coat of pearl pink lipstick. Shrugging, she winked at her reflection in the mirror. "What we women do for the men."

Walking into the kitchen, her eyes automatically flew to the clock above the stove. *Better hustle,* she admonished herself. *They'll be here any minute.*

She had just finished setting the table when a knock on the door announced the arrival of the two men.

"Come on in," she called as she removed the electric cord from the brown crockpot and transferred it to the middle of the table. "Bud, why don't you show your friend where to wash up, and I'll have dinner on in a sec."

When they re-entered the kitchen, Lareana was pulling a pan of warm rolls from the oven. Bud sniffed appreciatively. "That smells mighty good, Miss Lareana. Trey here thinks I come to deliver hay, but really I come for some of your good homemade bread. You downright spoil me."

"Didn't notice any cut in the price of hay." She slipped the rolls into a waiting basket. "And, Bud, I haven't officially met your friend here." Shifting her basket, she put out her hand. "I'm Lareana Amundson." Tall at five feet, eight inches, she still had to tilt her head back to meet the warm blue gaze of the man towering above her. He seemed to fill the room.

"Just call me Trey." His big hand enveloped hers.

"Hey, Lareana, where's John tonight?" Bud asked as he pulled out his chair. "Down in Portland with the show string?"

"Oh, Bud, you didn't know?" Lareana bit her lip. "John died last April . . . a car accident. . . . The other driver was drunk."

The pain sliced through her again, though, thank God, it came less often now. Convulsively, she clenched the hand holding hers.

Trey watched as the sparkle dimmed in Lareana's smiling face. He tightened his grip on the hand he still held, seeking to still its sudden tremor. He was surprised at the powerful urge he felt to take her in his arms. Talk about pluck, this lady had it. Even as he watched, her determined chin rose, a deep breath drained the tension from her shoulders, and she gently disengaged the hand that clutched at his.

"I'm sorry," he said and immediately felt helpless. What good would that do? What could anyone ever say to make a difference in a situation like this? She was so young, too young to suffer such a loss.

For once, Bud was speechless. Lareana glanced at him, saw the tear in the corner of his eye, and filled in the silence. "Bud, I'm the one who's sorry . . . to spring the news on you like that. I forget sometimes that everyone doesn't know."

He got to his feet and patted her shoulder awkwardly. "John was a fine man, made his daddy proud, he did."

Lareana shook her head. If only . . . but she knew by now that the "if onlys" always got her in trouble. She had to play the game the way it was dealt her. Her rose-colored glasses had been shattered with the night arrival of the state patrolman and had been buried along with her husband.

"Come on, you guys." She set the rolls on the table, but before she could pull out her chair, Trey was there, seating her, gently brushing her shoulder with a compassionate hand before seating himself.

Lareana bowed her head for grace and took another deep breath. This was just one more time when she missed John's resonant voice. "Thank you, Father, for the food we have and the friends we meet. Amen."

She glanced around the table to make sure everything was in order and encountered the intent gaze of the man sitting across from her. His look conveyed no pity, only the deep empathy of someone who has also suffered and therefore understands. She nodded. And felt comforted.

"If you'll pass your plates, I'll dish up the beans. The pot's too hot to pass." She opened the crock with a potholder.

Bud cleared his throat. "Your Uncle Haakan helping you then?"

"Yes." She scooped up a ladleful of the beans and the rich molasses sauce onto his plate. "He does most of the chores, but he and Aunt Inga had a community Grange meeting tonight. I talked them into going out for dinner first, though. He needed a night off." She held out her hand for Trey's plate. "When it's not raining, Johnny and I don't mind milking at all."

"This looks delicious." Trey motioned when he had enough on his plate. "I can't remember when I've had real baked beans. I thought they almost always came in a can."

"Awww-w, not this woman." Bud spoke around a mouthful of beans and fresh rolls. "She's the best cook in the county! Cooks from scratch, too. You oughta taste her rhubarb pie."

"That a hint, Bud?" Lareana smiled.

"No, no, 'course not," he sputtered, with a sly look and a wink at Trey, "but then again. . . ." All three joined in the laughter at his innocent expression.

"Oh, I haven't offered you anything to drink," said Lareana apologetically. "What'll you have?"

"I'd like a beer," Bud replied, "if you got it, that is."

"Not anymore." A frown puckered Lareana's smooth brow. "I won't have liquor of any kind on the place. As far as I'm concerned, it can all go —"

"Okay, okay, I understand." Bud braced his elbows on the table. "Just make it coffee, tea, whatever. . . ."

"Guess that's getting to be my soapbox," Lareana admitted. "But too many people are killed or have their lives really messed up by drunk drivers. Somebody's got to do something about it."

And I'll bet you're just the one, Trey thought, admiration for her growing by the moment. *I'd hate to be on the opposite side of any battle with you.* He tried to shake off the invading argument: *But people can drink and still function. You can't tell the world to lay off the booze.* He wiped his mouth with a napkin and arranged his silverware on the plate in front of him. "Thank you, ma'am. That certainly was delicious."

"You'll have coffee and dessert, won't you? Even if it isn't rhubarb pie?" She winked at Bud as she scraped the plates. But before she could get to her feet, Trey was beside her, removing the stack and setting them in the sink. She hesitated a moment, unaccustomed to such chivalry. Setting and clearing the table had always been her job.

"Where are the cups?" he asked, turning to face her as she set the bean pot on the counter.

"Up there." She pointed to the mug rack hanging on the end wall of the oak cabinet. "Do you take cream and sugar?"

He shook his head. "Just black."

She poured three cups of coffee and Trey helped carry them to the table.

"Seconds of dessert, anyone?" she asked when the men's plates were cleaned in record time. "I have nearly a whole pan of apple crisp left."

"No, thanks." Trey shook his head.

"Me neither." Bud eyed the pan. "But I sure wish I had some more room. That was mighty fine." He pushed his chair back and reached for his hat. "We gotta be hittin' the road. It's a long way to George."

"Are you going back over the Pass to-night?"

"Yeah. If I get too tired, this young buck here can drive. Thank you, Miss Lareana. And . . . and I'm sorry, truly sorry for what you've been goin' through." The catch was back in his throat.

Trey extended his hand and his clasp was warm and firm. "Thanks for the meal. I'll see you again." His words were more state-ment than question.

Lareana nodded. "Drive carefully now." The scene seemed to unfold in slow motion as he lifted his hat, secured it over his wavy, roan-red hair, and finally released her hand.

That's some pair, Lareana mused as she leaned against the open door frame until she heard the gate latch click. *Mutt and Jeff.* She chuckled to herself when the floodlight picked out the two broad-shouldered men. Within moments the green semi rumbled past the fir trees, a blink of the headlights bidding her goodbye. How thoughtful. If he'd tooted that air horn, Johnny might have awakened, screaming his head off. She closed the door.

By the time she had the dishwasher loaded and the kitchen cleaned up, she heard her young son squirming in his crib, making the tentative noises that would soon cre-scendo into loud demands for food. She gave the blue tile counters a last swipe before entering the baby's bedroom. In the light from the door, she could see him turn to watch her, his chubby fists waving in the air.

Following their familiar routine, she shrugged into her blue robe and slippers, pulled a dry sleeper on over the baby's downy head, and settled once more into the carved rocking chair by the fire.

Lulled by the flickering firelight and the nursing infant, her mind slipped back in time. Like a benediction to the day, the memories came . . . flooding her with warmth and peace. Memories of John were painfully sweet. She had met him on the fair circuit, when as young 4-H'ers, they had shown their fathers' registered Ayrshires. Everyone had said they were too young for marriage.

While they waited, there had been cooking school and courses in restaurant management for Lareana.

She and John were best friends as well as lovers. After the wedding, they had combined their growing dairy herds, leased a farm with an option to buy, and began building their future. Neither of them was afraid of hard work, and it began to pay off. Two years later, they signed the purchase papers on their land.

Folks in the tiny community of Yelm, Washington, spoke of them with growing respect. John was no longer Sig Amundson's boy, he was young Amundson, an influence to be reckoned with. Lareana, too, was making a place for herself in her adopted community. She became president of the local homemakers organization and her 4-H club was becoming famous for its award winners.

The baby's arrival fulfilled all their dreams. Johnny. She nuzzled his head, breathing in the sweet baby smell.

How quickly their plans had come crashing down around them. That rainy April night . . . the patrolman saying John never knew what hit him —

Lareana was slowly aware of the tears slipping down her cheeks, the collie at her feet, the grandfather clock ticking away in the hall, the babe fast asleep in her arms. "Ah, John," she murmured to the picture on the mantel, "everyone says I've handled all this so well. Then why am I so lonely at night? When will the tears be over?" She closed her eyes, her head resting on the back of the rocker.

Unbidden, the more recent memory of a tall stranger intruded into her thoughts. And the refrain from "Some Enchanted Evening" echoed faintly in her ear, whistled by a man who filled doorways.

Two

The following morning Lareana did the customary feeding at the calf barn, carrying Johnny in a navy blue pack on her back. Hanging the nipple buckets in front of each bawling calf, she spread out grain for the heifers already weaned. His own tummy full, Johnny waved and chortled at the animals.

When she took the buckets back to the milk barn to wash them out, she found a white-haired, slightly stooped giant running the milking machines. "Morning, Uncle Haakan. How was your dinner last night?"

"Inga, she liked it." The rhythm of his speech, along with arctic-blue eyes, echoed the land of his origins.

"And you *didn't?*" Lareana could not resist poking a bit of fun at the scarcity of his words.

"Umm-mm."

"Was that a yes or a no?" She turned to

28

pour disinfectant in the buckets, then scrubbed them briskly. After a good rinse, she tipped them over a rail above the deep galvanized wash sinks. "The hay haulers came last night. A new man . . . Trey somebody . . . came with Bud."

Uncle Haakan mumbled something under his breath, too low for Lareana to hear.

She looked up quizzically. "You've been down to the barn?"

He nodded again.

"Want me to wash up for you?"

He shook his head. "Inga will have breakfast soon. You go on up."

Apparently she wasn't going to learn anything much about the evening from her taciturn uncle. She should have known.

The morning sun was quickly dispelling the bite in the air as Lareana and her small passenger strode across the narrow field separating the two houses, the collie bounding at her side. An early frost had set the vine maple by the drive exploding with vivid scarlet, flame, and vermilion. Spiders, artisans of the night, had decorated the hog-wire fencing, now bejeweled with dewdrops that refracted sunbeams like fine prisms.

She walked backward a few paces so she could see her mountain, etched white against the deepening blue of the sky.

"Oh-h, baby mine," she whispered to Johnny, "God's world certainly is grand this morning." She shifted the straps biting into her shoulders as she prepared to climb the sty. Johnny squealed and kicked when she jumped down lightly, pausing to catch an extra lungful of the pure air. "Hey, we're gonna have to put you in a stroller if you get any heavier, young man!"

Aunt Inga's green thumb was evident in the profusion of fall asters and mums bordering the sidewalk and surrounding the double-wide mobile home when Lareana arrived at her uncle's home. Hanging baskets and planted pots of lush greenery turned the deck into a veritable greenhouse. Lareana pulled off one boot, then the other, at the bootjack and opened the sliding glass door. She was greeted by waffle and bacon perfume and the song of a canary, who was trilling his heart out in the corner.

"My, the roses are certainly blooming in your cheeks." Inga, a snow-capped dumpling of a woman, reached to help Lareana remove the backpack. "And how's my little man?" She hugged the baby to her. "Umm-m. Such a big boy now."

"Sure smells good in here." Lareana sniffed the mouth-watering aromas.

"Uncle Haakan won't be up for a while

yet. He wouldn't let me hose down for him." She turned on the water in the sink to wash her hands, then leaned back against the tile counter as she dried her hands with a towel.

Aunt Inga had taken Johnny on her lap. While removing his hat and jacket, she kissed each tiny palm and patted them together. The baby answered in jumbled sounds and stuck one finger in her mouth to be chewed on and growled over. His giggles became belly laughs, deep for a baby, and as catching as a yawn.

"Sure know where I rate around here these days," Lareana teased, lifting the lid of the cast-iron skillet to check the bacon.

"Here, you take him." Inga hugged Johnny once more, then handed him back to his mother. "I'll pour the batter in the waffle iron. There's water on the stove for tea if you'd like some."

Lareana strapped the child into the high chair that always stood ready by the maple table, then accepted a plate for herself when the delicacy was done to a golden turn.

"Aren't you having any?" Lareana asked around a mouthful of waffle drowned in homemade blackberry syrup. She speared another slice of bacon and leaned back on her chair to munch in comfort.

"I ate early. Besides, I'm still full from dinner last night."

"Good food, huh?"

"We went to that new Surf and Turf in Tacoma. I think Haakan would have been just as happy at the café in Yelm, but I enjoyed myself." Inga sat down at last and sipped her coffee. "My land, they have this flaming-up grill where you watch your dinner cooking and a lobster tank — you should see the size of some of those things — claws fit to —"

"You had lobster?" Lareana's voice rose to a squeak.

"No, no. We just *looked at* them." Inga patted her hand. "They're much too ugly to eat."

Lareana shook her head. "I suppose you had ground round or —"

Inga tried to look offended, but the twinkle in her eyes belied the effort. "Halibut. About the best piece of fish I've ever eaten, too. You know, I refuse to buy steak. Our own are better. Besides, we wouldn't waste the money on —"

"I know, I know, Aunt Inga." Lareana laughed, having heard all her aunt's arguments many times before, then changed the subject. "Was the service as good as they say it is?"

"Yes, but the prices —"

"I thought the motto of that place was "Great food, great service, at 'roll-back-the-years prices.' " Lareana recalled the TV commercials advertising the new place.

"Humpf. They certainly didn't roll the years back very far. But then we didn't used to go out much, either. Haakan has always preferred to eat at home."

Lareana stirred from her comfortable chair with regret. "Speaking of which, I'd better get in gear. I have all kinds of chores waiting at home, and it looks like our young friend here is ready for a nap." Johnny yawned and fought to keep his eyes open, then jerked upright when the phone rang.

"Good morning. Three Trees," Inga answered, then turned to Lareana. "It's for you, that real estate fellow," she added in a stage whisper.

Lareana took the phone, her brow arched, and spoke into the receiver. "Good morning, Mr. Horton. I sure hope you have some good news for me today." She listened for a few moments, her face lighting with a mega-candle smile. "Just a sec." She covered the receiver with her hand. "Can you watch Johnny at about eleven? Mr. Horton says he has a buyer for that freeway parcel."

"Of course."

33

Lareana returned to the phone. "Yes, I can make it. I'll be at your office at eleven. Umm-hum. . . . 'Bye now." She whirled in place as the phone clattered back in its cradle. "I'll be there with bells on!" She hugged her aunt impulsively, then herself. "Come on, fella, we gotta hustle!" She removed the tray from the high chair and scooped the baby out.

"Why don't you just leave him here with me now?" Aunt Inga asked. "That would give you some extra time."

"Sure you don't mind? I don't want to take advantage —"

Inga wrinkled her nose. "Oh, child. Having the two of you around is what keeps us young. You get going now." She nestled the sleepy baby against her shoulder. "And I have plenty of your milk in the freezer for him. You won't need to hurry back."

Lareana kissed Inga's wrinkled cheek and then her baby's smooth one. "Thanks again."

By the time she'd pulled her boots back on, sprinted to the sty, and balanced on the top board, she could contain her exuberance no longer. "A buyer!" she shouted at the crow in the top of a fir tree. "Hear that? We've got a buyer!" Samson barked, not sure whom she was talking to. Lareana leaped as far as she could, arms waving, ponytail bouncing. She hit the ground at a run, the sable dog at her side. *Wonder who it is?* The question crossed her mind when she stopped to open the aluminum gate. She shrugged it aside. *Who cares? Just so he has tons of money.*

"This is as bad as going into the show ring," Lareana muttered to herself as she parked her decrepit Datsun in front of the real estate office. She'd dressed the part of a successful businesswoman — tailored navy wool suit with a pearl-pink blouse. The pearl studs in her ears had been a gift from John one Christmas.

With a quick glance in the rearview mirror, she tucked a strand of golden hair back in the loose knot she had fashioned atop her head. More lipstick. A dusting of powder over her nose. "You're stalling," she admonished the direct blue gaze in the mirror.

With a deep breath, she slung her navy leather bag over one shoulder and stepped from the car. *Lord,* she prayed silently, *if I'm not doing the right thing, You slam all the doors . . . hard . . . so I know for sure what You want.* She eyed the pink polish she'd applied to her rounded nails. *But let me get my fingers out of the way first, okay?* Her quick grin toward the fleecy clouds was a soft amen.

A gray-haired man looked up with a smile when she walked in the door of the real estate agency. "I'll be right with you," he said as he finished his telephone conversation, giving Lareana a moment to study the seascapes on the walls. One — a sailboat, with red, white, and blue striped sails full and running before the wind — caught her eye. Someday she would do that, she promised herself. Sailing like that must feel like taking a horse over a jump — free and lighter than air.

Mr. Horton, his telephone business finished, put a stop to her daydreaming.

"Mr. Bennett should be along any moment now. Can I get you a cup of coffee or something?"

Lareana shook her head. "He's already seen the property then?"

"Yes. We went out this morning."

"And . . . ?"

"And, ah, here he is, right on time."

Lareana turned, following the direction of the realtor's gaze. Strains of "Some Enchanted Evening" whispered in her mind as her eyes widened in surprise.

The three-piece gray suit definitely did more for Trey than plaid shirts and worn jeans, but either way, he made an impact.

"Lareana Amundson, I'd like you to meet George William Bennett the Third, owner of the Surf and Turf restaurant chain."

Lareana extended her hand, but the greeting was stuck in her throat somewhere along with her carefully cultivated poise.

Her hand disappeared into his, its warmth familiar.

"I'm glad to meet you, Mr. —"

"Trey will do just fine. How would *you* like a moniker like George William Bennett the Third?"

She shook her head, a spark of mischief peeking from beneath dense lashes.

"Trey?"

"As in three the third. Trey to all my friends."

"So which is the real you? The hay hauler from last night or —" She paused to stare pointedly from his shiny wing-tipped oxfords up to the perfectly creased pants, marking the maroon and navy striped tie and the way the tailored jacket hugged his broad shoulders, then bringing her gaze level with his — "or is it the Wall Street executive?"

"Both. Neither. I don't really haul hay anymore. But Bud needed a helper, and I wanted to see how that end of the business was progressing."

"So you spent three hours unloading alfalfa, about six more in the truck, and you're back here this morning. Don't you ever sleep?"

"Some. These old bones didn't want to get up this morning, let me tell you." He massaged the muscles in his upper arm. "That's one job that'll keep you in shape."

"I take it you two know each other?" Mr. Horton observed dryly.

"Yes." Trey shifted his attention back to the realtor. "Did you know this lady makes the best apple crisp around?"

"Can't say I've had the privilege." Horton opened the half gate and indicated two chairs by his oak desk. "Won't you be seated?"

Trey placed his hand in the small of Lareana's back and ushered her before him.

Feeling as if she were one step off in a precision-marching band, she allowed him to steer her to the plush wing chair. The farmhand last night had been easy and relaxed, as comfortable to be around as an old shoe. This man, the owner of Surf and Turf, was known all over the Pacific Northwest as an up-and-coming tycoon, no doubt a wealthy one. One part of her resented the fact that he'd taken advantage of her, might even be laughing at her now. But she looked up to find warm blue eyes silently appraising her, and she realized that no ulterior motives were hidden there.

Trey watched the thought patterns crossing her face like clouds on a summer's day. He could tell she was fighting feelings of discomfort, confusion. *Come on, Lareana*, he begged silently. *I'm the same guy you met last night. Don't let the titles fool you. And money doesn't mean a thing. Be open like last night.*

He hadn't been able to get her out of his mind. The long truck ride last night had given him plenty of time to think, to dwell on each word and nuance.

She was a special woman. He wanted to know her better.

Lareana turned to the realtor as he seated himself and shuffled the papers on his desk.

"As I said, Mr. Bennett has already seen the property, Lareana." He turned to Trey. "Why don't you tell her what you have in mind?"

When he'd left home this morning, Trey had planned to make an offer considerably below the asking price, but not now. He was almost certain Lareana Amundson needed the money badly, or she wouldn't be selling. The parcel of land was a legacy from her grandmother, Horton had told him.

The sight of one pink-tipped finger massaging the knuckles of the other hand clenched in her lap decided him. "I'd rather show you," he said. "Do you have time to drive out there? We can talk over lunch."

He had a habit of turning questions into statements, Lareana thought, recalling his words of the night before. Now she barely had time to wave at the man behind the desk before Trey was leading her out the door and handing her into a sleek, silver Corvette parked at the curb. The maroon interior enfolded her as he settled her into the deep leather seat and hooked her seat belt.

"Whew!" Lareana whispered to herself as he slammed her door and rounded the front of the long, sculptured hood. "A steam roller is subtle compared to this man!"

"Comfortable?" Trey fastened his own seat belt and glanced at her before turning the key.

"Yes." She slid one hand down over the edge of the seat, luxuriating in the smooth grain of the leather. She sniffed the aroma of fine car interior mingled with just a hint of after-shave, a citrus-woodsy blend. She closed her eyes for a moment, enjoying the sumptuous atmosphere. A tiny chuckle, a fairy song, escaped before she could stop it.

Trey watched her. He seemed to be doing a lot of that when she was around. She was all woman — one only had to look at her to know that — but her charm lay in that childlike wonder, her unabashed enjoyment of everything around her. His hand itched to tuck an errant strand of spun gold back into its fashionable knot. Twenty-four hours ago, he hadn't even known her. Surely love at first sight was only for the movies or in books. Surely. He closed his eyes, cautioning himself. He would have to take it slow and easy with this one.

"Why don't you show me the fastest way?" The turn of the ignition key brought the engine roaring to life. "I'm hungry."

Lareana gave instructions with only half a mind. When they were finally on the freeway and heading south, she leaned her head back against the headrest. Both the powerful car and its owner, who seemed suited for just such a machine, made her feel pampered and petite. It was an unusual feeling. All her life, partly because of her height and solid bone structure, she had been considered capable, competent, a leader. Her forthright manner only added to the illusion she had created, an illusion that had become a reality with the passage of time.

She felt anything but capable today, however. Selling land she had owned only a short time but that had been in the family for years was not on her normal agenda. But then, since John's death, she had been doing all kinds of things she had never expected to do. Good thing she had the faith to believe that God knew what he was doing, even when she didn't. A funny little muffled sound escaped, hovered in the rich air, and before dissipating, reached the ears of the man behind the wheel.

"Why the sigh?"

"I don't know." She shrugged, then added, "Too many changes, I guess."

He wanted to reach out and take her hands in his, to still the fingers that were still worrying the knuckles on the other hand. All his long-buried protective instincts surfaced as he saw her struggle to hide the tension.

"Change can be a positive thing."

"True. But sometimes I feel caught in the eye of a hurricane. Things are out of my control, things I didn't plan for, didn't anticipate. Didn't even want."

"Like —"

"Like John's death, of course, for one thing. Like selling this property for another —"

"You're getting a good price for it."

"Am I?" Talking with him in the warm cocoon of leather, she felt as if she'd known him all her life. She watched him from beneath lowered lashes, trying to concentrate on the business at hand. Instead, here she was, baring her soul.

"But you see, I've never owned anything before. No, that's not strictly true. I owned my cows. But this is land. There's something —" she stopped to marshall her thoughts — "something about owning a piece of land that's permanent. You may be able to change the top layer, but it will always return to its natural state, if given the chance. Land is *real.*"

"That's why I still have my ranch at George. Guess you and I are farmers at heart. The land is part of us." He shifted his gaze from the ribbon of concrete to smile at her, an intimate smile that drew them closer. "Lovers of the land."

She nodded.

"I'm going to buy your property." He turned his attention back to the road.

"Just like that?"

"Just like that."

"No dickering? I thought you were supposed to make an offer, and I'd make a counteroffer. I'm all prepared."

"I've already left a down payment with Horton. We can close the deal by the end of the week."

The enormity of what he was saying hit her like a shower of sparklers and lit her eyes with miniature candles. He was going to buy the land! She gave a decidedly unprofessional bounce in her seat. Visions of new dairy stock, mortgage notices marked "Paid," and badly needed repairs vied for first place in her head.

"Lareana?"

"Hm-m?" She wrestled her thoughts back from the farm and focused her attention on the man beside her. Impulsively she laid one hand on his arm. "Thank you, Trey. You have no idea what this means to me."

He felt the warmth of her hand through his jacket sleeve and turned to smile into her glistening blue eyes. But his gaze strayed to her mouth, which was slightly atremble with the intensity of her feelings. The urge to stop the car and take her in his arms was overpowering, and he had to clench the wheel with both hands. *Slow down*, cautioned his brain. *Don't forget to take it slow. She has no idea how you feel.*

"You're welcome," he said. "Want to know what I plan to do with it?"

"Sure." Lareana realized she hadn't inquired into his plans at all. All her thoughts had been on herself and her needs. She was instantly contrite. "I don't suppose you want to farm it?"

"No." He took the exit to Tenino, turning the car into the service road at the property line after they crossed the freeway. He stopped, switched off the ignition, and leaned muscular forearms on the wheel, staring out at the flat ground covered with pine and tall fir trees. A rusty barbed wire fence sagged in some spots, was nonexistent in others. One of the ancient cedar fence posts leaned drunkenly on the wire for support. He turned to look at her. "Have you ever been to Knott's Berry Farm?"

"Yes." Lareana's puzzlement showed on her face. "Years ago. Why?"

"Because this —" he made a sweeping gesture — "is Timber Country."

"Those trees aren't big enough to log yet."

"No, no! Timber Country will be a theme park. All my life I've dreamed about a park like Disneyland or Knott's Berry Farm here in the Northwest. We'd have a log ride through a timber mill and lumber town, a lumberjack museum, skid rides behind mule teams, a family restaurant. All the other rides could imitate logging procedures —" He shoved open his door. "Here, let me

45

show you."

Lareana blinked as he slammed his door and rounded the car. A theme park? What a dream. Here? "But it rains all the time," she said as he opened her door. "At least, it rains a lot of the time. How can you build something like that here?"

Before she could question further, he had tucked her arm in his and was leading her through the knee-high grass to the straggling fence.

"The restaurant would be over there." He pointed to an area dominated by ancient stumps with young trees growing from them. "We'd need a huge parking lot. The log ride would start right between those two giant firs. I'm going to keep as many of the original trees as possible."

"Trey!" Lareana laughed as his enthusiasm caught her like a whirlwind and lifted her off the ground. She tried seeing the site through his eyes, but rain clouds kept obscuring her vision. "But what are you going to do about the rain?"

"Rent umbrellas. Build covered walkways. I don't know, but I do know I can make this work." He hugged her to him with one arm around her shoulders. "One of my favorite writers, Dr. Robert Schuller, says, 'Dream big. God honors big dreams,' so

46

that's what I'm doing. Can't you just see it?"

Once, as a teenager, Lareana had been to Knott's Berry Farm. There hadn't been many sightseers, so she and a friend had ridden the log ride again and again. She could still feel the thrill of the last steep swoop and the swoosh as they hit the water's surface. "You'd build all kinds of logging scenes for the log ride?"

"It could be an historical ride from early days to modern methods. I don't know. I have to think about that. But there has to be a place where the loggers blow a logjam apart. I've been recruiting people from Disney and Six Flags. I've told them my dreams, and they're drawing tentative plans. We meet again next month."

"Next month? But you don't even have the land yet."

"I know."

"You're crazy."

"Yup. Certified . . . certifiable . . . which is it?"

"I don't know." Lareana felt bubbles of laughter welling up within her. "I don't care!" She paused, her gaze roving over the property. "Timber Country."

She chewed on her lip, thinking hard. "Have you ever ridden on a Percheron?"

47

The question took him by surprise. "No, why?"

"I've always wanted to ride elephants, but here you could sell bareback rides on Percheron horses — the bigger the better. And Smokey the Bear could walk around greeting the kids and . . . and —" Her gestures grew wider. "Are you going to have Paul Bunyan and Babe the Blue Ox and — ?" Her words tumbled over each other.

"In the rain?" He turned, smiling down at her. Her face was flushed with the bloom of excitement.

"So sew monstrous ponchos!" She flung her arms wide to encompass them all.

Trey threw back his head, his deep laughter rolling over the rocks and Scotch Broom. He grabbed her with both arms, his hug lifting her feet from the ground.

Without another thought, he bent his head and planted a laughing kiss on the softness of her uptilted lips.

THREE

In the exuberance of the moment, the kiss didn't register in Lareana's mind even when Trey set her back on the ground. They stood, arm in arm, and surveyed the land, both dreaming the dreams of what could be.

"Can't you just see it?" he asked. "I've been imagining it for so long, it's like the finished product in my mind. I can hear kids shouting and bands playing, chain saws roaring and even a rooster crowing."

"A rooster crowing?" Lareana turned to him with question marks in her eyes.

"Sure. There'll be a petting zoo, Ole's Barn. They had to have milk and eggs and stuff at the logging camps. Besides, a rooster is nature's alarm clock and —"

"And — ?"

He grinned at her like a little boy with his hand in the cookie jar. "I just like chickens, banties especially. I'll have families of them

49

running all over the park. You know, males of every species could take parenting lessons from banty roosters. They —"

"A chicken man!" Lareana shook her head, trying to keep from bursting into gales of laughter. "And banties at that! Somehow I never pictured —" She covered her mouth with one hand.

Trey assumed an air of injured dignity. "You can be assured, madam, that I will not buy you chicken for lunch." He offered his arm with a bow. "Shall we go?"

At the solemn look on his face, Lareana lost her composure. Peals of laughter broke forth, startling a blue jay watching them from the safety of a nearby alder. She tried to stop, but one look at Trey as he saluted the scolding jay caused her to hang onto his arm and bury her face in the gray wool of his suit coat.

Trey kept his own response under tight control, but his eyes delighted in her joy. When she raised her face, the urge to wipe her tears away with his fingers swept over him. Instead, he pulled out a snowy handkerchief.

"In the books, the hero dries the suffering maiden's eyes." He tipped up her chin with one hand and carefully blotted the moisture from her sparkling eyes. "I have a feeling this is a portent of things to come."

"Meaning — ?" Lareana swallowed another giggle. She clamped her lips together, but her eyes refused to give in.

"Meaning our friendship . . . we're *both* crazy."

"Thanks a lot. Just because we're a cowgirl and a banty boy!" She placed her hand dramatically over her heart.

Trey drew himself up to his full six feet, three inches. "Banty boy? I resent that, ma'am. You're calling *me* little?"

"No, no. I meant banty . . . as in chicken."

"So . . . I'm a *chicken.*"

Lareana shook her head, chuckles still escaping like feathers after a pillow fight. "I give up." She raised her hands in mock surrender.

Trey tucked her hand back in the crook of his elbow. "Let's go eat."

Once she had won the battle of the seat belt and the car was roaring its way back up the freeway, Lareana let her mind float back to the scene at the property. It felt good to laugh again, to share a joke with a man, an attractive man at that.

She touched her fingertips to her lips. Such a simple gesture — a kiss. So long since her lips had been warmed by another's.

She shifted her gaze to the man beside her. Relaxed as he was, the power in his muscular body was only leashed, not tamed. His hands, bronzed from hours in the sun, held the wheel with an easy touch. His only jewelry was a square-cut black diamond on his right hand. Scattered hairs escaping immaculate shirt cuffs caught the sunlight and glinted fire.

She studied his face, a friendly face but with a square jawline that spoke of bulldog tenacity. His nose would be classic except for the slight bump, maybe a memento of childhood scuffles. The sight of sculpted lips reminded her of shared tenderness — lips turned up in laughter, lips touching hers —

With a breath that frilled her lungs and further relaxed her shoulders, she leaned her head back against the plush seat and allowed her eyelashes to drift shut. Everything felt so good — the car, the man beside her, the sale of the property, the money to expand Three Trees. . . . But what about the price? They'd never really discussed it. How did one gracefully bring up a subject like that? Her eyes flew open as her mind toyed with the options, and the musings sent shadows flitting across her forehead.

"Tell me about yourself." Trey broke into her concentration. "Start way back."

Lareana thought for a moment. *What could a man like Trey want to know about her?* "I've always lived on a farm, loved my freedom, my cows, a horse. Oh, and my family, of course."

"Where did you go to school?"

"Well, I grew up over by Puyallup —"

"I meant college."

"I started out to get a Home Ec degree at WSU, but when I realized how much I liked specialty cooking, I transferred to Willamette Institute's chefs' school in Portland."

"I've hired several people right out of that school. It's good. Did you go to work somewhere then?"

"Three Trees. John and I were married right after school. I practiced on him. But if I could be a chef in a really good restaurant and never leave my farm, I'd be perfectly happy. The two don't seem to fit, though."

"If the dinner last night was any indication —"

"That was nothing. I just threw some beans in the crockpot and whipped up an apple crisp. I use a lot of apple recipes since we have so many fruit trees. Entered one in a contest one time."

"And you won first prize?"

"Nope. Honorable mention." She turned

to face him. "I'll have to make it for you sometime."

"I'd like that. Did you come up with that recipe?"

She nodded. "I experiment sometimes, and I really like collecting old recipes. Some of them I adapt, others I keep in a file. Someday I'll put together a cookbook. They tell you a lot about the life and the people way back when."

"Have you ever cooked for crowds?" The seed of an idea sprouted in the back recesses of his mind.

"Just hot dishes and stuff for potlucks. That's always a good place to try something new. You get immediate feedback. If they don't like it, you take a full pan home. Why?"

"Oh, just a thought. How does lunch at the Falls sound?"

"Great." She tightened her lips, but the grin refused to be hidden. "Are you sure there's something besides chicken on the menu?"

A few minutes later they were seated at a window table overlooking the narrow Tumwater River. The water cascaded over stairstep falls, swirled between boulders, and paused in shallow pools before rushing to meet the southernmost tip of Puget

Sound. In the county park off to the side, two children played on the swings while their mothers visited at one of the picnic tables.

A man, hands clasped around bent knees, sat on one of the flat rocks jutting over the spilling waterfall. Off to the left, the Olympia brewery towered above the hillside.

Lareana's feelings of contentment grew until they flooded her inner being.

"Welcome back," Trey said softly when she finally turned to him.

"It's beautiful, isn't it?" A tiny smile played at the corners of her mouth.

"Watching water in motion always has a soothing effect on me. I love the music of rivers and creeks, the rhythm of the ocean. There's a creek back of our woods where John and I used to go for picnics or just to sit and relax."

"I'd like to see it someday." Trey recognized in himself a growing need to bring her peace and contentment, to see that tiny smile flirt with the corners of her mouth, to share more moments like these with her.

She smiled dreamily. "It seems you've pulled the stop on all my secrets. Now it's your turn."

"First, what have you decided to eat? Our waiter is coming."

Quickly she scanned the menu in front of her. "I think the shrimp-stuffed sole with a spinach salad. Iced tea to drink."

"What about chicken cordon bleu —" A passerby would never have recognized the dig from the serious look in his eyes. Only a tiny muscle twitching in his cheek betrayed his mirth.

Lareana wrinkled her nose at him but refused to rise to the bait.

As he gave the order to the waiter, her attention wandered back to the scene in the park below. A man had joined one of the women and her child. Then with the tot between them, stretching up to hang onto his parents' hands, the family ambled away toward the parking lot.

A swift stab of sorrow pierced Lareana's mood. She and John would never swing little Johnny between them, would never tumble him through the leaves, or teach him to pump a swing high to the heavens. She chewed on her lower lip, fighting to keep the tears from sneaking around the lump in her throat.

You will not cry, she ordered herself sternly. She swallowed hard and blinked to banish the threatened overflow.

Trey watched her silently, immediately aware of her distress and the cause of it. All he'd had to do was follow her gaze to the little family walking across the parking lot.

If only I could say the magic words for her, he thought, *I'd make it all go away.*

"A wise man once said," he began softly, reaching one hand across the table to cover hers, "that a burden shared is halved and a joy shared is doubled. Earlier we doubled our joy. Now . . . let me walk through this with you, too. Tell me how you feel."

Lareana turned her hand, clutching his strong, warm fingers. "It still hurts," she whispered. "When I saw that family down there . . . I know better . . . but that could have been John and Johnny and me in a couple of years. Sometimes I get so jealous I want to scream. I want to shake people and tell them not to take what they have for granted." The tears turned her eyes to pools like those in the river below, shimmering in the sunlight on the surface, but hiding secrets in their depths. Her fingernails bit into the palm of his hand.

"I'm afraid taking things for granted is normal for most people."

"I know. And now I think it's one of our worst offenses." A tear lurked at the edge of her lashes, in spite of her control. "I have to remind myself that God knows what He's doing, because I sure don't."

"Do you blame God for John's death?"

She pondered for a moment. "No . . . it's not that. God didn't make that man drink himself senseless and then drive a car. Bad things happen in this world. But I always thought they happened to *other* people."

"To someone you don't know," he prompted.

"Yes, that's part of it. I guess I *did* blame God at first." She stared down at the salad plate that had appeared before her, then lifted her eyes to his. "Sometimes I even blamed John for leaving us. Isn't that silly?"

It was all Trey could do to remain in his seat. All of his instincts were to take her in his arms and try to absorb some of her pain, to shield her from the past. He'd never felt this way before.

"No, not silly. Just part of the grieving process." His thumb gently stroked the side of her hand. *I know how you feel, gallant lady,* he thought. *One loses, on either end of marriage.*

Lareana took a deep breath. Calm returned to her face, chasing away the tension, covering her sadness. She lifted her chin a fraction, in a gesture Trey was discovering meant, "I can handle it myself now."

"Thank you." She squeezed his fingers lightly, then released them. Picking up her napkin, she placed it in her lap and folded her hands over it. Obviously the time of sharing was over.

Trey watched her compose herself. He saw only golden threads swirled into the knot on top of her head as she bent to give silent thanks for the food. With her the gesture was completely natural, part of her being. Trey found himself thanking God more for the woman across the table from him than for the food.

They continued to eat in silence, but it was the silence of two people who have shared something important and are secure with each other and with themselves.

Half an hour later, when they were back in the car, Lareana leaned against the seat. "Thank you for both the lunch and the shoulder."

"You're welcome, and while it may sound trite, please know the shoulder is available at any time." Trey crossed his arms on the steering wheel. "My father died years ago. While I hurt a lot, I remember my mother crying for what seemed like forever to my young mind. I had thought that men aren't supposed to cry, but one night she heard me sobbing into my pillow. She held me and I held her, and those tears — the ones we cried together — seemed to make things better from then on."

When he turned to look at her, Lareana felt her heart tug at the sight of moisture filling his eyes. She reached out her hand and laid it over his. This time it was his turn to accept a gesture of comfort.

Guiding the Corvette back toward the freeway, Trey said, "I've got an idea, and while I keep trying to push it to the back of my mind, it refuses to leave. Want to hear it?"

"Of course." He had definitely pricked her interest.

"Would you bake up some of your apple recipes and maybe some of the old ones you've collected?"

"Sure. When?"

He consulted his pocket calendar. "How about a week from Saturday?"

"Why?"

"I'd like to sample them."

Lareana thought for a moment. "Then why don't you come early and stay for dinner, around six?"

"It's a date." He eased his car into a parking place by the real estate office. "Lareana, I paid the asking price for your place. Sign the papers as soon as Horton has them ready, and the check will be waiting."

"I can't begin to thank you —" She stared at him, wanting to say more, but unsure of how to express the churning emotions. She just knew she was glad she would see him again.

Lareana flung open the door of her aunt and uncle's home. "The property sold . . . for the full price! Can you imagine that?" She greeted her aunt with a mighty hug. "Now we can go buy some cows and fix up a bunch of stuff around here."

"Slow down, child." Inga patted her niece's arm.

"How was Johnny? Did he behave himself?"

Inga looked at her as though she'd misplaced a marble or two. "Our Johnny?"

"Of course. He isn't always the angel you insist he is." Lareana grinned. "He's been known to pitch a fit once or twice." They both turned as tentative gurgles signaled the baby's awakening. *Cinderella's back to normal,* Lareana thought as she went to pick him up.

The following Monday a tube-shaped package arrived in the mail. When Lareana opened it and unrolled the poster, she burst into laughter. A golden banty rooster, feathers cloaking his legs, clutched the top rail of a weatherbeaten fence. His flapping wings lent strength to his morning pronouncement. Lettered across the top of the picture were the words: "This is the day." The familiar verse concluded at the bottom: "which the Lord has made."

"I couldn't resist," read the masculine scrawl on the back, with the signature, "George William Bennett the Third."

Lareana taped the poster to the door of one of the kitchen cabinets. Every time she looked at it, she could hear the crow of a rooster, accompanied by the sound of laughter.

On Thursday a station wagon with a large red plastic bow adorning its roof drew up into the yard. When Samson refused to stop barking, Lareana had to go outside to quiet him. The courier got out, went to the rear of the car, and let down the tailgate. She grasped a knot of strings and began the tug of war to extricate a bobbing bunch of helium-filled balloons. One at a time, they bumped and straightened, hearts and squares and circles, a rainbow of colors cavorting in the sun.

Samson barked in a frenzy of warning as the courier handed the strings to Lareana. Hanging onto the balloons, trying to shush the dog, and somehow thanking the delivery woman between her own howls of merriment gave Lareana no time to read the card. She didn't have to. But later, she read the inscription attached to one of the balloons: "Saturday at 3. Trey."

Maneuvering the unorthodox bouquet into the door of the house posed another problem. Lareana finally tied them to the stair post — all but the one she fastened to Johnny's swing. The baby's eyes grew nearly as big as the balloon.

"As he said," she told the staring baby, "he's crazy." She shook her head at the riot of color, and at one balloon that had broken free and was bumping on the ceiling. "And who cares?"

By noon on Saturday, she was ready. Sourdough biscuits were rising on the counter. Homemade blackberry jam, apple butter, and honey from the Three Trees' hives filled the three crystal jars on the lazy Susan. Beef stew simmered on the back burner of the stove, the vegetables, carrots, and potatoes from her garden waiting their turn. She had thought about fixing chicken and dumplings, but couldn't bring herself to do it.

Blackberry cobbler would be ready for the oven when they sat down to eat, and her specialty, apple pizza, steamed on the rack, spicing the air with tart apple and pungent nutmeg.

As she sat curled in her chair with a cup of herb tea, Lareana rubbed Samson's back with one slippered foot, enjoying a rare moment of leisure.

When she had picked up Trey's check the day before, the sight of so much money had nearly unnerved her. What would it have looked like in cash? She smiled, imagining a stack of bills. The way things went around here, one of the cows would get out and start munching the stack away. The ridiculous picture brought a chuckle.

On the dot of three, Samson barked at the door. A car had driven into the yard. Lareana let the dog out.

"That's okay, Samson," she called as the tall, broad-shouldered man stepped from his car. "He's a friend."

The dog's plumed tail wagged in welcome, escorting the visitor into the yard.

Lareana waited on the porch, enjoying the scenery — man and dog. A navy pullover sweater hugged Trey's broad shoulders, his light blue shirt collar visible under the crew neck. Jeans rippled over his legs as he strode up the walk, but the smile stretching the corners of his mouth and lighting his eyes arrested her full attention.

In like manner, Trey relished the picture she made, framed by the porch posts. Her dusky rose sweater and matching slacks set her cheeks aglow and hinted at the pleasing curves underneath. Trey forced himself to greet her casually. He couldn't sweep her up in the embrace he imagined, not this time.

"Thank you for my house decorations," she said as he came up the walk.

"You're welcome." He stopped abruptly. "What smells so good?" His nose wrinkled in appreciation. He sniffed again, one foot on the bottom step. "Woman, how can you look so relaxed when my nose tells me you've been cooking your romantic heart out?"

"You asked me to use some of my recipes. I aim to please!"

He took her arm. "Let's see what you've been up to."

Johnny stopped his jabbering when he saw the tall man enter the door. Lareana stooped down to pluck the baby from the swing seat. As she rose with him in her arms, she made the introductions. "Trey, I'd like you to meet Johnny."

The baby stared at the man, glanced back at his mother, then waved a chubby fist, his toothless grin announcing his approval. He kicked his feet and twined his other hand in his mother's hair, all the while jabbering and drooling, his two latest accomplishments.

"I think I passed," Trey said softly.

"With flying colors." Lareana winced and reached to free her hair from the baby's fingers. When his attention switched to her gold chain and heirloom cross instead, it was easy. "Sorry, young man," she said as she put him back into the swing. She picked up an assortment of toys from the floor and dropped them in the tray. Johnny beamed up at her, then attacked them with both hands.

As Trey watched, envy, desire, and pleasure chased each other through the corridors of his mind. The picture surrounding him was all he'd dreamed of, his goal for a lifetime — a loving woman, a beautiful, healthy son, fragrances of cooking that spoke of caring, time to grow together. A prayer passed unbidden from his subconscious. *Somehow, God, make this mine. Please don't give me a glimpse of perfection and take it away.*

"Would you like to see what I've made?" The sound of her voice drew him back. "Or would you rather wait until dinner? I thought if you got here in time, we could go for a walk. I'd like to show you my farm."

Trey nodded. "I'd like that. What about Youngstuff here?"

"We'll just put him in his backpack. I'll even let you carry it."

Trey was amazed at the speed with which they were loaded and out of the house. It was obvious Lareana had done this many times. He paused on the step, adjusting the straps. Mt. Rainier beckoned in the east. Down at the barn, some of the red and white Ayrshire cows had started to line up for milking. Samson took his place as escort, every once in a while sniffing the hand of the man allowed to carry the dog's precious charge.

Lareana pointed out the sights as they ambled down past the barns and into the old orchard. An ancient log cabin was slowly sinking into oblivion in the shade of a huge walnut tree.

"That's a shame," Trey commented, pointing to the rotting frame.

"It was too far gone when we moved here. I would love to restore it, but that takes big bucks. The fruit trees are responding, however." She nodded at the trees branching above them. "It's taken lots of pruning and spraying. At first I thought we'd killed them, John cut them back so far. This year we got a good crop, especially the Gravensteins. Nearly every morning I can look out my kitchen window and see deer grazing here and farther down in the pasture. Once we even saw a bear."

The pastoral scene suited her, Trey thought, as he watched Lareana. The breeze had tugged strands of hair loose from the leather slide she wore and teased her face with the tips. Her sky-blue windbreaker matched her eyes and brought out the translucence of the skin over her cheekbones. His fingers itched to tuck back an especially determined sweep of gold.

"Lareana, do you want to hear about my idea?"

"Of course, but you make it sound so solemn."

"That's because it's really important to me." He shifted the straps as Johnny bounced in his carrier. Trey correctly interpreted her questioning look. "No, he's not bothering me. I need someone to develop a menu and specialty dishes for my restaurant at Timber Country. I thought of you." He raised his hand. "Now, hear me out before you say anything. I think I've covered all the bases."

Lareana nodded, locking her hands behind

her as they strolled back up the hay road.

"I want a distinctive flavor, as we've discussed. You already have a good glimpse of my dream, you collect the kind of recipes I want, and you're trained to cook for a commercial establishment. In addition, you said your dream —"

She nodded again. "I remember."

"You wouldn't have to leave the farm, especially in the early stages. You could do all the experimenting and researching from your kitchen. Then when we decorated, you could have a hand in that, too. What do you think?"

"You mean I can talk now?" Her grin erased the sting in her words.

"Only if you'll say yes."

They had reached the gate to the yard. Lareana swung it open, but turned to gaze at the mountain before she entered. "One thing I want you to know . . . I never make a major decision — and you must admit this would be major — without praying about it first. My inner reaction is, 'Yes! Yes! Capital yes.' But I have to consider what's best for Johnny, too."

"I thought of that. That's why I pointed out that so much of it can be done right here. I believe it will give an even stronger sense of the early days since you would be operating out of your own kitchen." He paused when her grin widened. "How am I doing?"

Lareana didn't answer right away, but turned and led the way into the house. "Would you like a piece of apple pizza to hold you over until dinner?" She lifted Johnny from the backpack and set him in the high chair.

"Apple pizza?"

She chuckled at the tone of his voice and offered a bribe. "I'll even warm it in the microwave for you. But come look before you make judgments you might regret later."

The pastry filled a pizza pan, but there all resemblance ended. Spirals of apple slices filled the thin pie crust. Crunchy topping finished it off, making Trey's mouth water.

"I think I love apple pizza!"

She sliced a wedge-shaped piece, slipped a paper plate under it, and set the microwave for thirty seconds. It was worth the short wait. After one bite, the only sounds Trey made closely emulated the gustatory satisfaction of a third-grader.

"I thought apple pizza might become a hallmark of your Timber Country. You know, with stands all around the park: 'Get your apple pizza here.' Like other parks have done with snow cones." She waited for his reaction.

Trey licked the pad of each finger with careful deliberation, then located a drip of topping in his palm. Finally his tongue cleaned each smidgen of flavor from his lips.

"You could always have another piece." Lareana nodded toward the pan, her voice breaking as she swallowed her delight. "I won't even charge you."

"Where did you come up with an idea like that?"

"I take it you like the product?"

"*Like* is an understatement. You, my dear young lady, have been hiding your talents under a bushel . . . of apples!" He settled back against the counter. "How much would you suggest we charge for each slice?"

"Well —" A hint of a frown creased her forehead as she pondered. "I'd thought maybe seventy-five cents, but I'm sure it could go for even more than that. I'd cut the pieces generously."

"Of course."

She glanced up to catch a ghost of a smile lurking in his eyes. "Are you serious about this or just leading me on?"

"I'm serious! I'm serious!" He held up his hand like a traffic cop halting oncoming cars. "It's just that I can't imagine your doing anything ungenerously."

71

"I think that's a compliment."

"I think you're right."

"Then . . . thank you."

"You're welcome."

He's so good for me, Lareana thought as she cut him another piece of the pizza. *I haven't laughed this much since . . . since I'm not sure when. He was right when he said we're both crazy. And I love it!*

The dinner hour came and went as Trey raved about all the different items Lareana had prepared. The sour-dough biscuits were a keeper, Trey commented, the kind of item that could be unique. And the blackberry jams and cobbler. Well!

"I have no doubt," he said as they finished clearing the table, "that you could put together a prize-winning menu." He stopped her with a hand on her arm. "Lareana, please. Really think about my proposal. List all the questions you come up with and we'll discuss them. I know you caught part of my dream —"

The pull to answer yes right then was almost overwhelming. It would be a real challenge, one that she'd have to work into an already crowded schedule. She had enough to do on the farm. But . . . maybe . . . by hiring more help . . . and winter was slow anyway. . . . Working with Trey would be fun, too, and designing a restaurant was something she'd always dreamed of. In fact, his dream dovetailed with her own. But she had said she would pray about it, and she would. That was the bottom line. Wouldn't it be nice if all this *turned out to be God's will in action?* a small voice whispered from somewhere deep down inside.

"Thank you for your vote of confidence." She smiled up at him. "Let's go dream in the other room where it's more comfortable."

Johnny immediately nuzzled against her when she picked him up on her way into the living room. "Hungry, hmm?" She turned the tape deck on, picked up the baby's blanket draped over the back of her rocker, and settled herself down. As she leaned back, one foot automatically reached to twirl the stove handle, and strains from *South Pacific* filled the room.

"Have a chair," she pointed to the other rocker in front of the wood stove. She snuggled the baby down in her arms and covered him and her shoulder with the patch-work blanket.

Samson left his spot at Lareana's feet and padded over to lay his muzzle on Trey's knee. Trey obliged, stroking the sleek head. The dog sat at his side, requesting, never demanding attention. A brass floor lamp with a Tiffany shade in rusts and yellows occupied the space between the chairs. An oak magazine rack flanked the more masculine chair, while a basket with yarns and crochet hooks sat beside her own.

I've come home, Trey thought. *I belong here. John, thank you for this gift. I promise to take good care of them. They won't want for anything, I assure you. We have so much love to share.*

Trey turned his attention back to the woman across from him. Lamplight and firelight vied for the privilege of bathing her in their glow.

Feeling his gaze, Lareana looked up from her contemplation of the infant in her arms. It seemed so right. The man in the chair across from her, one hand stroking the dog. *He cares for us!* She felt a small shock. She had never thought about another man coming into her life. John was the only man she had ever wanted.

Wasn't this too soon? John hadn't really been gone that long. Or did feelings take time into account? *God, you must have brought Trey into my life for a reason. Guess I'll just have to wait and see.*

She felt a smile leave her heart, lift the corners of her mouth, and wing across the warm air, asking admittance to the heart of the man. Nothing was said. Everything was understood.

FOUR

The following morning Lareana had a hard time concentrating on her chores. Her mind kept dancing back to the evening before. She and Trey had put the baby to bed, then sat in front of the fire sharing all the important events of their lives. They had so many mutual interests — Rodgers and Hammerstein musicals, frosty nights, the smell of new-mown hay, riding a good horse through the early morning dew. And both of them loved the mountains.

She knew now how he could relate to her sorrow. His pain had been caused by losing a woman who decided she hated both him and his farms.

"We got engaged right out of high school," Trey had said. "We were starry-eyed and sure we had the world by the big toe. But I was determined to make that farm a paying operation before we married. The longer we waited, the more Jane decided she couldn't stand living 'out in the desert' as she called it. And since I didn't feel I could live anywhere else — besides the fact that our livelihood would come from those hayfields she hated — she left."

Lareana watched as the memories flitted across his face. "Did you try to persuade her to come back?"

"She refused to talk with me. Why, I didn't even know where she was for a while." Trey clenched his fist on the arm of the rocker.

"That must have been hard."

"Mostly on my pride." Silence reigned, but for the hum of the blower on the stove.

Lareana tapped the floor with her toe as the rocker moved gently.

"The funny thing is," Trey continued, his eyes staring into space, "it was not long after that, I entered the restaurant business. Now I have a condominium in Seattle. I don't spend all my time there, but I can't stay at the farm in George all the time either. As far as I can tell, I have the best of both worlds."

"And it doesn't hurt anymore?" Lareana leaned her head against the back of the rocker, watching carefully for any signs of pain on his face.

"No. I've come to realize how different we were. I don't think —" He leaned forward, hands clasped on his knees. "Have you ever known someone who just couldn't seem to be happy? As if nothing was ever good enough or large enough or shiny enough?"

Lareana nodded.

Trey shrugged. "Now all I feel is sorry . . . for her, for people like her. I like making people happy, Lareana. That's one of the joys for me with Surf and Turf. People come to my restaurants and get away from the things that bother them. Just for a little while, they're happy. Timber Country will do the same thing."

Lareana watched the glow from the fire play games with the shadows across his face. *This is a man,* she thought, *who dreams big. He doesn't just stop with wishing. He goes after what he wants.* Yes, Trey would make his dreams become a reality.

"You've made *me* happy," she whispered across the space between them. And it occurred to her that she wanted to make him happy, too.

Lareana finished feeding the calves and didn't remember a bit of it. A soft glow suffused her face, lending extra color to her cheekbones. She wasn't aware of it, but Uncle Haakan recognized the symptoms right away. But he never said a word.

As she neared the house, Lareana's steps slowed. With a shrug, she adjusted the backpack. Johnny had fallen asleep, and his dead weight caused the straps to bite into her shoulders. Turning at the gate, she glanced toward the mountain, but low clouds shrouded the peak.

"Father," she continued the prayer that had been on her mind all night and all morning, "what is it You want me to do? Is this job with Trey in Your will for us? It seems so to me. It came out of the blue, something I wanted but hadn't slaved and planned for. Sometimes I wish You would speak through a bush again —" she eyed the rhododendrons lining the fence — "or on the wind. . . . Somehow, I have to know exactly what You want." She waited as if hoping for a sign. The breeze stirred the tall firs behind her and lifted the tendrils of hair, fanning her face, but there were no words she could understand.

A sigh seemed to start in her toes and work its way up. Johnny stirred, a tiny whimper reminding her she had other things to take care of. Samson nudged her hand with a cold, wet nose. The scent of wood smoke drifted down from the chimney on the tall white house, calling her back to what she had in the here and now. A second sigh, this time lighter and only from her diaphragm, turned into a whisper. "Patience has never been one of my virtues, has it? Thank you, Father, that Your plan is already in motion. Just clue me in when I need to know, all right?"

The breeze chuckled through the trees overhead.

Prayers for knowledge of the Father's will floated on both her conscious and subconscious mind for the next couple of days. During her devotional time, Lareana searched the Scriptures for some indication of what direction she should go.

When she allowed her mind free reign, she could picture the restaurant, taste the good things on the menu, and hear the customers laughing and having a good time.

Trey's words came back to her: *I want to help people be happy, even if only for a little while.* It seemed as good a reason as any for a business.

Finally, one morning, she called her mother. After the customary greetings and questions about the baby, a silence fell. Lareana cleared her throat. "Mom, how can I know what God wants me to do in a given situation?"

"What's wrong, dear?" Her mother's warm tones quieted the pounding of her daughter's heart. Lareana had heard that exact question many times in her life. But this time she hadn't told her folks about Trey's offer. She had told them about selling the property and about the buyer but —

Lareana took a deep breath. "I've been offered a job, designing a menu for a brand-new restaurant and helping set it all up. The owner —"

"Who?"

"Who what?"

"Who's the person who offered you this job?" Margaret Swenson's voice was quietly insistent.

"The same man who bought the freeway property. Remember, I told you he wants to build a theme park there — Timber Country. It will have a family restaurant." The words spilled out in her enthusiasm. She finally wound down, "And I can do most of the preliminary work right here, so I wouldn't have to leave Johnny or the farm."

She waited, knowing her mother was praying at this very moment. Lareana had learned from her mother long ago that there was no need to rush.

"Oh, babe." The childhood endearment came softly over the wire. "You have so much to do now. How can you think of taking on one more thing?"

81

"But, Mom, this is what I went to school for, a dream I've had for years. You know that."

"Yes. I know."

"But that's not the real question," Lareana persisted. "How can I tell this time what God wants me to do? Besides, with the extra money from the sale, we can hire some more help around here." She stuck the last in as an afterthought.

A chuckle warmed her ear. "Remember what Pastor Benson said that time? 'God can only guide you when you're moving.' Maybe this is one of those times when you'll have to step out and pray He will close the doors if you're going the wrong way."

"But I don't want to make a mistake."

"No. But then we learn by our mistakes, too."

"Hurts more that way."

"Yes."

"Are you saying I should try it then?"

"Have you made a list of all the arguments for and against?"

"Yes. There's a lot to be said on both sides." Lareana mentally reviewed the lists she had compiled the night before. "They seem to balance each other out."

"Then the question here is what's best?"

Lareana's smile lent love to her reply.

"Mom, that was the question in the first place."

"Well, if it doesn't violate anything in Scripture, if you've prayed to be in God's will, I guess —"

"The answer is . . . step out."

"Right. But be prepared to change course if God closes a door."

"And get my fingers out of the way — quick!" Lareana could picture her mother's warm smile as the familiar chuckle again reached her ear. "Thanks, Mom. I love you."

"Bless you, babe. Keep us posted."

Lareana hung up the receiver. Now to get in touch with Trey. His instructions came back to her. "Call my secretary. She always knows where I am." He had stuck his business card on the corkboard by the phone. Lareana stared at the embossed gray card for a moment, indecision skittering through her mind like maple leaves before an autumn wind.

Johnny called her from the bedroom, his awakening voice changing from a gentle query to a specific demand.

Lareana welcomed the interruption. "Coming, son." She went into the bedroom and picked up the squirming baby. "Good grief, you're soaked!" She held him away from her shoulder until she could lay him on the changing table. The aroma of baby powder soon filled the air, along with his contented coos.

Lareana settled Johnny on his tummy in the middle of a large quilt on the floor before she reached for the phone again. This time nothing stopped her as she dialed the Seattle number.

"Surf and Turf Enterprises," a professional-sounding voice answered.

"May I speak to Mr. Bennett?" Lareana asked, her fingers clenching the receiver.

"Who may I say is calling?"

"This is Lareana Amundson."

The voice immediately warmed. "I'm sorry, Mrs. Amundson, but Trey isn't here right now. He'll be calling in any time. But he said to give any message from you first priority."

"Thank you. Tell him I'm at home." Lareana hung up the phone with a twinge of disappointment. Was this some kind of answer to her prayers? Was she not supposed to take this job after all? Maybe Trey had changed his mind and didn't really want her for the position. The doubts grew with every passing moment.

"Stop it," she commanded her runaway feelings. "You're making Mt. Rainiers out of molehills."

It was evening before Trey returned her call. Just the sound of his voice in her ear brought her worries back to sea level. "I'm glad you called."

Trey cradled the phone against his shoulder and spun his chair so he could look out over Puget Sound from his tenth-floor office.

Seattle had donned her evening finery, including the diamond necklaces circling the blackness of the Sound. A ferry, on its hourly traverse between Bremerton and Seattle, sparkled like a brilliant emerald-cut jewel against the velvety darkness. Trey rubbed a tired hand over his eyes as he listened to Lareana's soft voice in his ear. The tiredness vanished in an instant.

"You accept? You mean you'll really do it?" His voice rose with excitement. "Oh, Lareana, this is fantastic. What a team we'll make!"

He listened a moment, a grin creasing deep valleys in the tanned skin of his cheeks. "No, I don't presume to play God, but I really felt this was meant to be. Thank you." He glanced at his calendar. "How about if I take you out to dinner tomorrow night? We can talk over the arrangements, salary, that kind of thing."

"Why don't you come here instead?" Lareana pushed her bangs to the side as she cradled the phone on her shoulder. "I could fix a picnic lunch, and we could ride out to the back forty by the creek." She felt a momentary twinge. The swimming hole had been one of hers and John's favorite spots. Did she really want to share it with a new man? She took a deep breath. "Bring your swimsuit if it's a hot day."

"What else can I bring? Salad? Dessert? How about some French bread and cheese?"

"Bread and cheese will be fine. See you about three?"

"Two, if I can make it by then. And, Lareana, thanks for the invite."

Lareana replaced the phone, her mind already on what she would serve the next day. She attributed the rising bubble of excitement and the grin she could feel dancing with the sparkle in her eyes to a chance to cook something special. It couldn't be the guest himself. Or could it?

By the time Trey arrived the next afternoon, Lareana had dinner stowed in a backpack and two saddle bags. She had debated on whether to take Johnny along, then opted for a call to Aunt Inga. Yes, she would gladly babysit for her favorite grandnephew. Lareana hugged both of them as she ran back out the door, delight in her freedom, in the ride ahead, and in her new friend lending springs to her feet.

"Any room for this?" Trey eyed her as she sat between the packs on the porch.

He handed her a wrapped package, then stepped back to take in the whole picture.

Sunbeams seemed trapped in her hair, and wild roses bloomed on her cheeks. Her smile of welcome flashed brighter than the sun. A blue plaid shirt, knotted at the waist, and rolled-up long sleeves showed off both the sky-blue tank top underneath and the golden tan of her arms.

"You look like pieces of the sun and sky came earthbound just for my enjoyment," Trey said softly.

Lareana looked up from finding a place for the extra package. "Why, thank you." She slipped the leather strap through the buckle. Her smile widened. "You don't look too bad yourself."

She saw that the *Gentleman's Quarterly* look had been exchanged for one straight out of *Western Horseman*. She rose and handed him the filled backpack, then whistled for Samson as she hoisted the saddle bag over her shoulder.

"I've already saddled the horses up in the corral." Lareana closed the gate behind them.

"How many horses do you have?" Trey asked as he settled the backpack in place.

"Three. My mare, Kit — she's a Morgan-saddlebred cross — and John's quarter horse gelding. He used Mike for rounding up the steers and cows."

"Mike?" Trey's eyebrows nearly disappeared into his hat brim.

Lareana laughed. "John believed in basic names. Nothing fancy."

"That's two."

"The third one is that little Welsh mare down in the pasture." She pointed to a small gray figure west toward the woods. "We bought her when we found out I was pregnant. John thought we should breed her when the baby was born so the colt and kid could grow up together. Maybe I'll still do that."

Thoughts of John's dreams that had crashed in the fatal collision took over for a moment. She couldn't always find the enthusiasm to make them happen without him. Like getting the mare bred. Time whipped by like a whirling dervish. She was so busy trying to keep up that the extras, the special things they had planned together, often didn't get done.

Trey resisted the urge to interrupt her memories. He watched her face carefully, ready to intervene if she needed him. He, too, remembered stillborn dreams.

They reached the aluminum gate to the corral without breaking the silence. Both horses nickered when Lareana spoke to them. She handed Trey part of a carrot. "Give Mike this carrot, and he'll love you forever." She pointed to the bay with a white blaze who had his head turned expectantly. The deep sorrel mare beside him flung up her head and slammed an impatient foot into the dust.

"Easy, girl." Lareana rubbed the horse's satiny neck and palmed a carrot for her mare. "You need a good run, don't you?" The mare's answer was a sharp nudge in the chest.

"A bit high-strung, is she?" Trey unclipped the lead shank and turned Mike toward the gate.

"Not really. Just has a mind of her own." Lareana finished, tying the saddle bags down. She checked the girth for tightness and swung aboard. "Dad says she's mean clear through, but I've always been able to handle her. I like the challenge, I guess. Besides, she has the easy gait of a saddle-bred, pure heaven to ride." She leaned forward to hug both arms around the mare's neck. "You old sweetie, you." The mare nodded and pulled on the hackamore, ready to go.

On the ride to the creek, riots of scarlet vine maple screamed, "Look at me." Tall elms and firs shared their flickering sunlight and shadows with the errant breeze whispering secrets in their branches.

Trey drew in a deep breath of air, redolent with fir spice and falling leaves. He leaned the heels of his hands on the saddle horn and raised himself in the stirrups, both knees and elbows locked. "Ah-h-h-h." His whoosh of escaping breath spoke his delight as mere words never could.

A cock pheasant called from back in the underbrush. Lareana searched carefully, finally able to point him out, nearly invisible in the foliage surrounding the stump he perched on.

"This certainly is different from the hills around George," Trey said. "The only trees on a thousand acres are the ones I planted myself. But they'll have to grow some to beat this."

Lareana tried to see the overhung logging

road through his eyes. "Guess this is another one of those things I take for granted. But I love it out here. Any time. Any season. There just never seems to be enough hours in my day. Gotta check the fence lines soon."

The chuckling creek announced itself before they rode into view. A grassy glade banked one side while the other side hid under the drooping maples. Sunlight bounced shafts of diamonds off the ripples and peeked into the shadowed nooks and crannies, transforming the moss to emeralds.

"Just drop your reins. They're both trained to ground tie." Lareana swung out of the saddle and unknotted the latigo securing the saddle bags. "If you want to swim, the hole is on the other side of that enormous elm." She caught the questioning arc of his eyebrows. "I'm just wading today."

"Too cold, huh?"

"Well —"

He shrugged out of the backpack. "Even I'm aware that this is October, and you've already had a frost here. Let's just eat and wade. And especially the former."

Later, after they'd frozen their feet in the creek water and devoured the gourmet dinner carefully packed in plastic containers,

91

Lareana retrieved two cans of pop from the creek and handed him one. A comfortable silence dropped around them as they leaned against a moss-covered root and watched the play of light and water.

"May I ask you a question?" Lareana turned to regard the man beside her.

"Um-m-m." Trey nodded without opening his eyes. "As long as I don't have to think too hard."

"How long did it take you to get over losing Jane?"

Trey pondered for a time. "I'm not sure. As the months passed, I found myself fretting about it less and less. I worked hard to keep any bitterness from developing, and I deliberately chose to forgive." He turned his head to look into her questioning eyes. "I found out that forgiveness means forgetting, letting go. And it meant forgiving myself, too. That was probably the hardest part of all."

"No 'if onlys'?"

"That's right. And no 'might have beens.' "

Trey wished he could tell her more about his newfound feelings, but he said nothing as he watched her lean her head back on the mossy root. *If only* . . . He smiled inwardly as he caught himself playing that game. *If you were ready to hear about the love I have growing for you. . . . One day,* he promised himself. *One day.*

"You know something I've missed the most?" She faced him again.

"What?"

"Times like this. Having a man for a friend. John and I were friends first."

She thought a moment. Talking of John and the experiences they'd shared made her feel good this time. Maybe the healing really was beginning. "Thank you." She laid her hand on Trey's.

"For what?"

"Oh . . . for talking, sharing." Her voice softened. "For being a friend."

The setting sun was casting deep shadows as they rode back to the barns and Trey said goodnight.

It was the next morning before Trey realized they still hadn't discussed anything about her job.

He made his phone call from the airport, since he had a flight to catch and wouldn't be back in town for a week. "May I take you out to dinner that Monday night?" At her answer, a frown replaced his grin. "Sure, we can make it an early night. Why didn't you tell me the trial was coming up?"

Lareana slumped in her chair by the phone. "I don't know. I guess I wasn't sure —" She chewed on her bottom lip. "Trey, this has nothing to do with you. It's my problem . . . well, not really . . . it's the law's problem. I don't have to go. I just want to. That man *must* be put behind bars before he can kill anyone else. His record stretches from here to next winter, and all because he drinks and drives." She stopped a moment to listen. "Yes, I'd like to have you go to the trial with me. As far as dinner goes, I'll see you about five that Monday. Thanks, Trey . . . for everything."

Lareana started getting herself and the baby ready early, but Johnny decided to help her out on the dressing table, kicking and laughing, making it nearly impossible to work his feet into the legs of his suit. Impatience was sneaking up on her, driving away the joy she usually found in the active baby.

"Johnny, sometimes —" She planted a kiss on his apple cheeks.

While she was still struggling with the fastenings, Samson's deep bark announced company. She picked up the baby and dashed for the door, at the same time mentally counting the things she had left to do. At least the apple pizza had come out of the oven, its nutmeg aroma wafting outward as she opened the door. Trey could snack on that while she finished dressing.

"I seem to make a habit of this," Trey greeted her. "But what smells so heavenly?" He sniffed again. "It couldn't be . . . apple pizza, could it?"

"Whatever happened to 'Hello' or 'It's nice to see you' or even 'Hi, Lareana'?" Her grin matched the one dimpling the baby's cheeks.

"Should I go back and start again?" Trey laughed, a rich baritone that caused the baby to wave his fists in delight. "My nose always seems to precede my mouth. Anyway, it's all your fault. You did the baking."

Lareana leaned against the door frame, resting Johnny on her hip. Her gaze ran appreciatively over the man in front of her. He had said "casual" but his casual look had come right out of the latest men's fashion magazine: what every well-dressed businessman wears on a date. Camel wool slacks were topped by a navy cashmere sweater. Its softness invited her to stroke the nap. One finger hooked the collar of the camel windbreaker slung over his shoulder. Her mind assessed all this in the minuscule pause between one breath and another.

"Would you care to sample while we finish getting ready?" She stepped back, inviting him to enter. "Youngstuff here hasn't been too cooperative."

"You look fine to me," Trey reached out one finger for the baby to grab. "I could take him for you, if that would help."

Johnny didn't hesitate as he was transferred from one pair of arms to the other. His mother managed to wipe the drool from his chin with a dishcloth just in time for him to lean forward and chew on the finger he gripped in one hand.

"Maybe I'd better wash my hands first, if I'm going to be part of the main course." Trey raised his eyebrows, the question mark intended for Lareana. She laughed as she left the room.

"Just remember, you asked for it."

Johnny continued his chewing as Trey snaked a chair out with his foot and parked in it. He transferred the baby to a place on his lap and laughed at the antics of the young charmer. Johnny responded with a belly chuckle of his own, but didn't release the finger of the man holding him.

"Ouch." Trey drew his finger back. "Lareana, he bites."

"Don't be silly," she responded from the bathroom. "He'll gum you to death but he can't bite. He doesn't have any teeth yet."

"Sure sharp for gums," Trey muttered as he pulled down Johnny's bottom lip. He paused, a grin deepening the creases in his face. "Want to bet?"

Lareana erupted from the doorway and pried open the baby's mouth. "He's got a tooth? Well, what about that? It broke through." Johnny twisted away, reaching again for Trey's finger. She dropped a kiss on his downy head. "Your first tooth . . . what a milestone. And you couldn't care less, could you?"

Her eyes met the lapis blue gaze of the man above her. "You don't need a Band-Aid or anything, do you?" she asked mischievously. "I mean . . . he did bite you." She chewed her bottom lip, trying to keep a straight face.

"Since I'm sure a tetanus shot is not in order, I'd settle for a piece of apple pizza, if it's not too much trouble." Trey tried to look soulful, but failed miserably.

Lareana got to her feet, her teal wool skirt swishing softly as she stood. "You're sure that's all you need? No coffee or tea or something to go with it? Maybe you'd like a topping of ice cream or whipped cream?"

"Enough. I surrender. Just get yourself ready, woman. Johnny and I have been waiting forever —"

Lareana shook her head again as she placed the slice of dessert on the table in front of him.

Trey glanced from her to the dessert to the baby in his lap and back to the woman standing in front of him. Both his hands were occupied — one holding the baby, the other in the process of having a finger shortened.

Lareana just shrugged her shoulders at his predicament and walked off. "Mothers use three hands all the time," she commented as she left the room.

When she returned a few minutes later — hair swirled into a loose knot on the top of her head and silver loops in her ears — Trey had found a solution. The apple pizza had disappeared, and now he was attempting to settle the gurgling Johnny in his car carrier. The baby even had a sweater and cap on.

Lareana watched for a moment as Trey bent over and nuzzled the baby's cheeks. One tiny fist tangled in his thick roan hair. Trey disengaged himself and kissed the tiny fist before rising to meet her eyes. "You two are something else," she said softly.

"Mexican all right?" he asked a few minutes later when they were all buckled in. Getting the baby's seat ensconced in the back had been no easy chore. The low lines of the Corvette precluded buckling ease, even for Trey.

"Fine." Lareana shifted her attention from the baby to the man beside her. "I haven't had a good chimichanga for a long time."

She ignored the countryside flashing by outside the car and let her thoughts roam instead. How much easier it was getting ready when there was someone else to help with the baby. Since she'd been a single parent from Johnny's birth, having another adult around was heavenly. She knew she could be spoiled quickly. Was God trying to give her some kind of hint? She really enjoyed being with this man, enjoyed not only his companionship but also his caring. But John hadn't been gone that long. She'd never planned a relationship with anyone else. Back to square one —

Let's face it, she told herself. *Johnny will need a male role model in his life, someone who'll teach him how to be a man.*

She gave herself a mental shake. What was she thinking of? Trey wanted to hire her to help with his restaurant, not marry her. But still . . . no, he was a friend, nothing more.

Los Amigos tried to live up to its name. The tables were so close together the patrons became acquaintances whether they wanted to or not. Obviously, the tiny café

99

was noted for its food and not for elegant atmosphere.

"We're in luck. We get a *booth*." Trey bent close to her ear to be heard above the mariachi recordings. They followed their hostess to a back corner where a large pink, bull-shaped piñata hung suspended over the table. When she set Johnny's car seat on the orange padded bench, he stared, entranced by the bright colors and the flickering candlelight.

"This is one of those places I've always wanted to come to and never took the opportunity." Lareana looked around, delight sparkling in her eyes. "I guess because I can't get used to going out alone. Thank you, Trey."

"Better wait to thank me till you've sampled the food. But the last time I was here, it was almost as good as what I had in Mexico City."

"When did you go to Mexico City?" Lareana asked over the top of her menu.

"A couple of years ago. I was toying with the idea of opening a Mexican restaurant, so I did some research." He glanced up at her. "Do you want something to drink? They make excellent margaritas."

"No, thanks." Her tone stiffened. "You know I don't drink, Trey."

"Do you mind if I have one?"

Lareana's forehead creased in a tiny frown. She started to say something, paused, took a deep breath, and started again. "I don't try to force my feelings on others. I . . . ah . . . I mean I know I can't change the world. But when John was killed, I swore I wouldn't drink again, that I wouldn't serve any alcoholic beverages in my house, and —" she stared at him across the table — "that I wouldn't ride with anyone who had been drinking."

"And you say you don't try to force your feelings on anyone else?"

Lareana straightened her spine and squared her shoulders. Her chin assumed its determined angle. "Is a margarita so important to you?"

Trey eyed her warily. "No . . . it's not. But I think you need to be realistic. People can enjoy a drink or even two and not suffer any ill effects. That doesn't make them drunk or drunkards."

"I know that." Though her voice grew softer, it still held a warning. "Can we drop the subject? Agree to disagree? I won't change my mind, and I have a feeling you aren't planning on changing yours, either."

Trey nodded, but when the barmaid

came, he ordered soft drinks for both of them.

"Thank you." Lareana smiled across the table at him, but the serious look never left his eyes. The piñata cast a shadow on his face, making it hard for her to read it. *Maybe this is what he looks like when business decisions don't go his way,* she thought. *I'd sure hate to be on the other side if he really got angry.*

"Have you decided?" His voice remained clipped.

"The chimi." Her smile entreated his return to their earlier enjoyment. "I've wanted one for a long time. They don't taste the same when I make them. But then, I'm not very good with Mexican food." Lareana felt she was babbling.

Trey struggled with his feelings. He hated to make her unhappy but . . . she was being unrealistic. And unfair. He'd never had an accident. In fact, on the few occasions when he'd had too much to drink, he had been wise enough not to drive. He wasn't stupid. He studied the face of the woman across from him. Flickering candlelight highlighted her cheekbones, sending her expressive eyes into shadows. The gold in her hair deepened into honey where the shadows fell.

I know you're coming from a difficult situa-

tion, he thought, *but I sure plan to do some-thing about where you're going. Somehow, Lareana love, you have to come to grips with the way the world is. People can drink and still function.*

He reached across the red and white checkered table-cloth and took her hand in his. His thumb stroked the fine skin, forcing her to relax. He watched as her shoulders dropped, the relaxation traveling up her arm and down to the toes of her shoes. *I love you,* he wanted to say. *Lareana, I love you with all I am capable of loving and then with whatever extra abundance God gives me.*

He took a deep breath. The time wasn't right. Not yet.

Johnny decided he was due for some attention, and interrupted their study of each other. When they ignored his suggestions, he switched to the demand that always got action. Immediately, his mother turned to him, her gentle voice belying the turmoil of only moments ago.

Lareana picked Johnny up, and reached for the diaper bag. "Bet you need dry britches, don't you?" Then, to Trey, she said, "We'll be back in a couple of minutes. Start without us if your dinner comes." She made her way to the restroom, grateful for the quiet when the door closed behind her.

On her return, a man from a nearby table stopped her. "Hi, Lareana." His flushed face testified to his diversion for the evening. "You finally come offa your farm?"

Lareana recognized one of the salesmen from the feed store. "Hi, yourself, Frank. It's nice seeing you. Enjoy your dinner." She continued toward her table with Johnny who was staring at everything from the vantage point of her shoulder. She thought she heard something about "widow-woman" from Frank's table, but she wasn't sure.

"Who was that?" Trey asked as she settled Johnny back in his car seat.

"A man from the feed store. He usually loads the truck for me." Her dinner had arrived and she bent her head for grace, then continued. "He's always been polite, kind of quiet. I was surprised when he stopped me."

Trey glanced back at the table where Frank and several of his buddies were ordering another round of drinks. One of them slapped the waitress on her derriére as she left to fill their order. She glared at them, then giggled. Trey glanced at Lareana, but she was engrossed in her dinner and had missed all the byplay.

Their earlier ease in conversation seemed to have escaped to the Bald Hills and refused an invitation to return. Trey finally pushed back his plate, his dinner half-eaten.

"Don't you like it?" Lareana asked. "Mine's delicious."

"Guess I'm not too hungry, after all. Want me to take Johnny while you finish?"

Lareana wiped her mouth with the napkin. "That's okay. I'm stuffed."

"Dessert, folks?" Their waitress stopped at their table. "Our flan is really good tonight."

"None for me, thanks." Trey smiled up at her. Lareana shook her head also. "Just bring me the check, please."

Lareana picked up Johnny and began to button him into his sweater for the trek home. Her first inkling of trouble came when a slurry voice interrupted her.

"If I'da knowed you wanted to go out, I'da called ya."

"What?" Lareana whirled around, her senses reeling under the miasma of alcohol fumes. "Just a minute, fella." Trey rose to his feet. "You have no reason to bother her."

"Buzz off, buster, I'm talking to the widow-woman here." Frank leaned both arms on the table, obviously needing the support.

"I said, 'on your way!' " Trey's voice deepened to a menacing growl. He grabbed the man's elbow with steely fingers and spun him away.

With surprising accuracy, considering his state of inebriation, Frank swung his other arm around and connected with the side of Trey's head. Only Trey's quick reflexes kept the punch from landing on his face.

"Stop it! Frank, you idiot!" Lareana felt waves of horror, generously spiced with pure anger, roll over her.

Two other men hustled the drunk out the door before anything else could happen. Trey glared after them, one hand rubbing the point of contact.

"Are you all right?" Lareana wasn't sure when she had gotten to her feet. She found herself standing in front of Trey, reaching with one hand to inspect the bruise.

"I'll be fine. That idiot was too drunk to do much damage." Trey waved aside the apologies of the manager and Frank's friends. "Are you ready?"

Lareana nodded, but before she could pick up the baby's seat, Trey had it in one arm, and his other hand securely around her elbow, ready to guide her out to the car. Two uniformed officers met them at the door. By the time Trey convinced them he didn't want to file charges, Lareana's anger was beginning to boil again.

"Why not?" she demanded as they drove

out on the street. "He needs to be taught a lesson."

"Granted." Trey's voice was still tight. "But I wanted you out of there . . . before someone really got hurt."

"But —"

"No buts. Do you want this kind of garbage spread all over the papers? That's what would happen if I pressed charges. I can't afford that kind of publicity, and you certainly don't need it."

Lareana stared at his clenched jaw and equally tight fists clamped around the steering wheel. "Trey?" Her question was tentative, seeking to soften the tension, as was the hand she laid on his arm.

"Oh, Lareana —" His voice broke. After a pause, he began again. "You could have been hurt . . . you and Johnny. I'd never have forgiven myself."

"It wasn't your fault."

"I took you there."

Lareana rubbed his arm and kneaded away the anger from his taut shoulder muscles.

"It was the alcohol," she said softly. "I wish —"

"Now what?" Trey thumped the steering wheel with the heel of his hand. Flashing blue lights were reflected in the rearview mirror.

FIVE

Trey checked the speedometer.

At the same moment, his foot came off the accelerator, but it was obviously too late. He couldn't argue. As soon as the Corvette rumbled to a halt on the narrow shoulder, he pulled his driver's license from his billfold.

Lareana watched, a tiny smile playing hide-and-seek around the corners of her mouth. When Trey glanced her way, she chased it quickly out of sight. Staring out her side window, she listened to the discussion between Trey and the officer.

It was a typical scenario. "Seventy miles an hour in a fifty-mile zone." The officer sounded stern. "What's your hurry?"

"I'm sorry, officer." The control was back in Trey's voice. "I guess I was thinking of something else."

Darn right, Lareana thought. *That fight back*

there would have broken anyone's concentration.

The officer took the proffered license and returned to his car. Silence held court in the Corvette while they waited for the verdict. Lareana tried to think of something to say, but the frown on Trey's brow precluded any easy conversation. The rhythmic thrumming of his fingers on the steering wheel intensified the silence until Johnny squirmed in his carrier. Lareana turned to rock the seat with one hand, appreciating the diversion.

"Thank you," Trey said as he signed the ticket. The officer had been sympathetic, reducing the speed to 65 so the ticket was only for speeding, not reckless driving.

"Now you take it easy, Mr. Bennett," the officer admonished. "Your family needs you around for a long time." As he strode back to his patrol car, Trey glanced at Lareana. "Family, huh?" He turned the ignition. "Sounds good to me."

Lareana felt the smile return from its hiding place as she watched Trey's right eyebrow arc and the corner of his mouth twitch. The stern look he'd worn for the last hour dissipated like fog in the sunlight.

"I've always wanted a knight in shining armor," she said, "but I never dreamed mine would ride up in a silver Corvette."

"Or fight for your honor in a Mexican restaurant?"

She thought back to the pathetic drunk taking a swing at Trey. Her smile died. "I hope someone is driving Frank home." She turned in the seat. "They wouldn't let him drive, would they?"

"The police probably booked him for drunk and disorderly conduct. He's sobering up in the cooler by now." Trey reached for her hand. "Don't worry. He's not out on the road."

"It happens so easily," Lareana mused after a time. Her fingers had finally relaxed in Trey's palm. "One drink follows another. . . . Nobody makes sense. . . . Those men were laughing and having a good time. Before anyone knew it, things got out of hand. I — I don't even want to face him the next time I go for calf feed."

"It wasn't your fault."

"I know that, but —" Her voice faded as she leaned her head back against the seat. Six months ago the trooper's voice had had that same air of authority. She heard his words again. "I'm sorry, Mrs. Amundson. There has been —"

Tears welled in the corners of her eyes and slipped silently down her cheeks. She swallowed, trying to dislodge the lump that suddenly blocked her throat. *Dear Lord,* she screamed in the quiet of her mind, *how can there be such joy and laughter one minute and such pain the next? Sometimes I wonder why You allow things like alcohol in this world. All it does is cause pain and unhappiness.*

"Lareana, let me in." Trey massaged the back of her hand with his thumb. "Share your thoughts, your feelings with me so I can help you."

She turned her face, and the light from the dashboard caught the shimmer of tears. "Trey, I loved him so. John was not only my husband, he was my best friend. Sometimes I —"

Trey waited for her to continue. He wanted to take her in his arms, to wipe away the tears and erase the pain. *A knight in shining armor,* he thought. *Maybe I can slay dragons but not the memories that cause her grief.* "Lareana, love."

He stopped his runaway thoughts as he realized what had slipped out. *Lareana, love.* Had she heard him? Would it make a difference? Love could make a difference, couldn't it?

He turned the powerful machine into the long, poplar-lined driveway of Three Trees Farm. Only Samson's half-hearted barking broke the silence when Trey turned off the ignition. He rested both wrists on the steering wheel, his square-tipped fingers hanging loose and relaxed. The beam from the mercury floodlight illuminated his features in sharp angles of black and white.

The light fragrance of her perfume teased his senses, and he closed his eyes for a moment, savoring the tiny whispers of her breathing, the warmth of her body so near and yet so far away. The officer's words came back: "Your family will need you for a long time to come." When would be the right time to acquaint Lareana with his feelings? She and Johnny were already his family, and he loved them.

Slowly he turned his head and looked into her eyes. Their warmth penetrated his thoughts. Anyone else would have questioned him, moved to gain his attention. Not this woman. She waited, giving him all the time he needed, giving him the kind of peace he'd been searching for, a feeling of coming home, of belonging.

He reached over the console and, concentrating all his love into the movement of his hand, picked up one of hers. He tipped his head forward and gently brushed his lips across the tips of her fingers. "I'll pick you up at eight-thirty, okay?"

She gave in to the temptation to stroke the wavy hair bent close over her hand. Her fingers threaded through its thickness, following the waves, brushing back the lock hanging over his forehead. It felt so right.

Trey closed his eyes, glorying in the thrills running down his back as her tentative touch grew confident. Angel wings grazed his forehead as she brushed back his hair.

"If you're sure you want to."

"What do you mean?"

"Well, I know how busy you are. . . . I hate to take up your time —" Her voice trailed off as his head snapped up.

"Lareana, do you want me there?"

"Yes."

"Fine. I'll be there." He opened his door, turning to wrestle the baby carrier out before Lareana could reach for it. *One thing I'm going to do,* he promised himself as he bumped his head on the door frame, *is bring the van when we take this young man along. Fitting Johnny and his paraphernalia in this car is the pits.*

Trey set the sleeping baby in the carrier on the kitchen table. Then he turned and tried to communicate all the love he felt into one hug. "Good night."

"Good night, Sir Corvette." Lareana hugged him back and stepped out of his arms. "See you in the morning."

Trey started out the door, but a thought caused him to turn back. "Lareana, at Timber Country you'll never have to worry about a scene like the one we just experienced. We won't allow patrons to get drunk. I promise you that."

Lareana shook her head. "Why should it be a problem there?" She stopped as the harsh realization dawned. "Do you mean you're going to serve liquor at the park?"

"Only beer and wine, no hard stuff. And it would be in restricted areas. I thought maybe applejack would be something different." Trey clamped his lips shut on any more explanations. The warm woman he had held moments ago had turned to glacial ice.

"I thought you understood. I cannot work for a place that encourages drinking." Winter had frosted her eyes. "Good night, Trey." She closed the door with a click.

Tears of disappointment ran rivers down her cheeks as she tucked Johnny into his crib. They dripped onto her night shirt as she crawled into her own cold, lonely bed. After blowing her nose for the umpteenth time, she plumped her pillow and shook her head. "Well, so much for that dream." She frowned at the moonbeams highlighting the oak flooring. This time the sigh came from her toes. *Wonder if I'll see him again, either? We're sure farther apart than I ever dreamed. Can't he understand —* Her musings were cut short by the ringing telephone.

A curt voice cut off her greeting. "Lareana, this has nothing to do with *us,* with *our* relationship. I won't let it. Now, in the past, we've agreed to disagree. Can't we do that now? Put all discussion of liquor at Timber Country on hold until I can do some more research?" He stopped, aware that she had not responded. "Lareana?"

"Yes." She felt a chuckle starting.

"Well?"

"I said yes. What more do you want?" She clamped her lips to keep the joy from spilling out.

Trey sighed, letting all the fear and antagonism drain away. She was being agreeable. They could work together. "You scared the living daylights out of me."

"Me, too. Trey, please understand how strongly I feel. . . . I — I can't work with booze."

"No more of this tonight. I'll see you in the morning. Good night, Lareana . . . love."

The dial tone buzzed in her ear.

A crowd had already gathered on the court-

116

house steps the next morning when Trey and Lareana arrived. Clouds scudded across the slate sky, harassed by the same wind that encouraged people to wrap their coats more tightly around themselves and seek the protection of doorways. Tired maple leaves plastered themselves on low-growing shrubs, hoping to end their dance of despair.

Lareana hunched deeper into the collar of her mauve down coat, grateful for its protection. The gray day matched her spirits. She had awakened that morning without her usual bounce, and as if that wasn't enough, Johnny had fussed when she left him with Aunt Inga. She told herself he'd be all right but. . . . The sight of her mother and father waiting in the hallway broke her train of thought.

"Oh, Mom." Lareana hugged the gray-haired, slightly rounded woman. But for the age difference, the two could have passed for sisters.

"It'll be all right," Margaret comforted her daughter.

"I'm Carl Swenson." The deep voice matched the size of the man, who patted his wife's and daughter's shoulders before extending his hand to Trey.

"I'm sorry." Lareana turned, embarrassment warming her cheeks already flaming from the wind. "Trey, meet my mom and dad, Margaret and Carl. Everyone calls Dad, Swen." Swen and Trey sized each other up as she finished the introductions, "George William Bennett the Third, Trey, to his friends." The smiles on the men's faces informed the two women of mutual approval.

Trey gestured toward the courtroom down the hall. "We'd better go in. They must be close to starting."

The jury had been selected the day before, so the trial was about to begin. But all the Perry Mason courtroom scenes hadn't prepared Lareana for the actuality. Only the color of the familiar flags broke the somberness of the wood-paneled room. The court reporter casually cleaned her glasses in front of the imposing bench against the far wall. All of the actors were in place and rose on command as the judge entered and was seated.

Silence fell like an oppressive cloud as the roomful of people found their seats and stared straight ahead at the drama about to unfold.

Seated between her mother and Trey, Lareana felt secure. Finally she had the courage to look at the man seated next to his lawyer at a table in front of the black-robed judge. Daniel Greaves was not a monster. Clothed in a dark blue suit with a white shirt and burgundy tie, he appeared the small town businessman he was. No red bulbous nose, no hangover slouch. Only the twisting of his thin fingers revealed his tension. Today the jury would have a hard time believing him to be the drunk his record proclaimed him to be.

"The state of Washington versus Daniel Greaves. The charge: vehicular manslaughter while under the influence of alcohol."

The judge looked at the man seated before him. "How do you plead?"

At the man's "Not guilty, your honor," Lareana felt a tiny flame flare to life in the region of her heart. She forced herself to sit still, even while the fidgets twitched at her arms and legs. As the trial progressed, the aura of unreality grew, and the tiny flame burned hotter and brighter.

This was the man who had killed her husband. And there he sat as if he hadn't a care in the world. When the judge agreed, "Objection sustained," Greaves smiled at his lawyer. When objections were overruled, the man only shrugged or didn't respond at all.

During the lunch recess, Lareana paid scant attention to either the food or the conversation. Trey watched her covertly as he became acquainted with her parents. What he saw made him uneasy, but it wasn't until the women left for the rest room that he got a chance to ask some questions.

"She took John's death extremely well," Swen responded to the first. "We figured it was God and her faith getting her through. But sometimes I thought she handled his death — the grieving and taking over the farm, the baby — almost too well. My wife says it was because farm women have learned to be strong, to recognize the seasons of life."

Trey nodded in sympathy. " 'A time to be born, and a time to die,' " he quoted.

Swen took another sip of coffee as if giving himself time to think. "It wasn't that she didn't cry and grieve . . . she did, but —"

Trey leaned forward, nodding again to encourage the other man's reminiscence.

"Sometimes grieving includes anger. Hers never did. She claimed she forgave the man —"

"But you don't think she did?"

"Time'll tell, Trey. Time'll tell."

Trey watched as the mother and daughter joined them by the cash register. Lareana answered when spoken to, but her usual

120

sparkle was as frozen as the ice in her eyes. Her chin held its imperial angle, secured in place by an invisible steel brace.

Back at the courtroom a small group of people had gathered in the hall, blocking the door. A powerfully built young man imprisoned in a wheelchair laid a hand on Lareana's arm.

"Mrs. Amundson?" His voice was polite but assertive.

"Yes?" Lareana paused. "What can I do for you?" Trey moved closer to her side, ready to intervene if needed.

"My name is Brian Campbell. This —" he gestured at his wheelchair and useless legs — "is the result of my encounter with Daniel Greaves. I was his first victim . . . I think."

Trey sensed rather than saw Lareana's reaction. He wanted to put his arm around her, offer her any encouragement he could, but her icy reserve screamed, "Don't touch!"

"I'm so sorry," Lareana said softly.

"I just wanted you to know that we want him off the highways as badly as you do."

Lareana raised her eyes to meet those of a young woman standing just to the right of the wheelchair.

"I'm Cathy Hanson. I spent three weeks in the hospital after that drunk ran a red light. I'm still fighting with his insurance company. Daniel Greaves spent six weeks in the detoxification center. He's back on the road."

"Why . . . why are you telling me this?" Lareana stared from one to the other.

"We're going to get him." Brian clenched his fist on the arm of the chair. "If Greaves is convicted on this charge, we'll be at the sentencing. Hopefully he'll be sent up for a long time. In the meantime, there'll be a civil suit."

"It'll cost him." Fire and threats flashed from Cathy's eyes. "It'll cost him plenty!"

Lareana nodded. Trey felt her trembling through the down coat. He gripped her elbow a bit more tightly and motioned her toward the door. They re-entered the court-room, finding their places just before the judge was seated.

Lareana kept her eyes focused on Greaves as the drama continued.

A state patrolman took the stand and introduced the evidence of a breathalyzer test. The level of alcohol in the defendant's blood was well above acceptable limits. Yes, he'd been drunk.

Greaves leaned back in his chair. Sometimes he scribbled notes on a legal pad. Never once did he appear regretful for his actions. It was as if someone else was on trial.

As the afternoon progressed, the tiny flame flickered and grew, licking up the sides of the cauldron steaming inside Lareana. Invisible even to those who loved her, it nonetheless began to bubble and spit.

"Forgive . . . that your Father may also forgive you." The Bible verse blew cool reason in through the windows of her mind, but instead of dousing the fire, fanned it more.

Forgive, Lareana thought. *What a joke!* The man had been forgiven over and over and look what had happened! More people had been hurt, maimed. *God, where were You when this was going on? What good did John's death do?* She forced her hands to remain folded in her lap. Cautiously she ran her tongue over her aching teeth. They had been ground together too long.

The angry cauldron finally boiled over when she reached the outside door after court had adjourned for the day. The trial would reconvene at ten in the morning. Prosecution was nearly finished.

"He killed John and injured those other people, and he doesn't even give a damn." Lareana ground out the uncharacteristic epithet. She rammed her fists deep into her

123

coat pockets, her navy pumps pounding out her venom as she descended the stairs.

A television crew was rolling their cameras as one of the reporters held a mike to Lareana's face. "How do you feel about the trial so far, Mrs. Amundson?"

Lareana never paused. "Hanging is too good for the man."

Above her head, Trey's and her father's eyes met. An imperceptible nod caused them both to take her arms and hustle her away.

"Later," Trey answered a persistent newspaper reporter.

Robotlike, Lareana followed instructions as Trey placed her in his car. She hooked her seat belt before folding her hands in her lap again.

"We'll follow you," Swen said as Trey walked around the rear of his car. "Margaret will stay with her tonight."

"Good." Trey nodded his approval. "I don't think she should be alone."

Lareana's responses on the ride to the farm were monosyllabic. No matter what Trey asked or said, Lareana refused or was unable to reply. Her mouth looked pinched, and her eyes vacant, as if she'd retreated to the far corners of her mind. One finger rubbed the cuticle of another. Back and forth. Rhythmically. The gesture accompanied the beat of the windshield wipers after the rain started to fall.

"I've never seen her like this," Margaret said after Trey settled Lareana in her chair before the wood stove and returned to the kitchen. Margaret dialed the phone. "Maybe when Inga brings Johnny over, it will help."

Lareana hugged the baby fiercely, as if he, too, might be snatched from her. When he started to fuss, she handed him back to her mother and went upstairs to change clothes to feed him.

Seated in her chair with the baby nursing contentedly, Lareana leaned her head back and closed her eyes. She could hear Trey and her parents in the kitchen, no doubt discussing her, the case. She didn't care. The steaming cauldron within had settled to a simmer . . . except for the moments she allowed herself to remember Daniel Greaves. Then the flames licked higher.

"I'll pick you up in the morning." Trey laid his hand on her shoulder.

Lareana nodded.

Trey paused as if searching for something else to catch her attention. With her eyes closed and the slumbering baby in the crook of her arm, she looked completely defenseless. At least the frozen look was gone. *Thank you, God, for small favors,* Trey prayed. *I don't know how to help her, so that leaves that ball in Your court.*

"Why don't you spend the night?" Margaret asked as Trey was about to go out the door. "It would save you some driving."

Swen nodded his agreement. "Then you could take both the girls to the courthouse in the morning. I have to go home now for chores. I could just join you in the courtroom tomorrow."

"There are plenty of beds." On any other woman, the look Margaret gave Trey would have been pleading, but on her it was the look of a gracious hostess.

"Thank you. I will." He opened the door. "I'll just get some things out of my car."

Dinner was a silent affair. Lareana pushed her food around her plate, then excused herself.

Trey helped Margaret clear the table, all the while engaging her in conversation. He found her sense of humor delightful, her common sense far above the norm. He could tell where her daughter's strength originated.

Lareana was back in her chair, the firelight painting golden highlights across her cheekbones and dancing sparkles in her hair. The tilt of her head shadowed her eyes. She might have been asleep but for the listless hand stroking the dog by her side.

Her mind kept returning to the wheelchair-bound man and the woman, Cathy Hanson. Their injuries were permanent, just like hers. No matter what happened to Daniel Greaves, life would never return to what it was before. Brian would never walk again. John was dead. And Johnny would never see his father.

But Daniel Greaves — He walked and talked and laughed and even drove a car. And drank. And smashed people's lives. And lived to drink again. And drive again.

Red fury misted the backs of her eyelids. The cauldron spat and foamed, threatening to overflow.

"It won't help, you know." Lareana heard her mother's voice as from a great distance. "I mean it, Lareana. You can't carry the burdens of those others. You can't even carry your own."

"I know. 'Let go and let God.' " Lareana's tone reflected the weight of the ages. She opened her eyes. "But, Mother, I've been doing that, and what has it gotten me?"

Margaret refused to answer the question.

I'd like to answer for you, Trey thought. *It's gotten you a gallant spirit that takes life's knocks on the chin and comes up laughing, a*

*son you adore, a man who loves you and
wants to take care of you, and a God who will
never let you go. Even though this plan B that
we're in is not the one you started out with, it
will be good. Believe me, Lareana, love.*

"You'll know again one of these days," her
mother said. "You'll know."

Lareana woke with the rending and smash-
ing of cars screaming in her ears. She
thought the whimpering was from someone
in the accident, but it was her own agony
that filled the quiet room. Samson thrust
his cold nose into the icy hand she dropped
over the side of the bed. When she didn't
respond, he pushed harder.

"It's okay," she murmured as she rolled
over, wiping the moisture from her forehead
on the pillowcase. "Good boy, Samson."
She rubbed his ears and muzzle. With the
fastest tongue in the west, he swiped the
salt from her cheeks. After she stroked him
one more time, he lay back down on the
rug.

Call on the name of Jesus, she commanded
herself. *Put Jesus in your mind, and there's
no room for nightmares.* Closing her eyes
again, she visualized the Man from Galilee
sitting on a rock beside a flowing stream.
Over and over she whispered His name,

"Jesus, Jesus, Jesus." Finally she sank back into oblivion, a smile now curving her lips.

Lareana awoke in the morning with the smile intact. The song had come back into her heart until the events of the day before resurfaced in her mind. She lay in bed, willing the image of Daniel Greaves to disappear. It didn't.

Keep Jesus in your mind, a tiny voice whispered in her ear. It had worked during the night. Why not during the day?

Lareana threw back the covers as Johnny's questioning voice called for a morning meal.

"One thing about babies," she muttered as she shrugged into her royal blue robe. "They demand to be fed no matter what's going on." She patted the region of her own growling stomach. "Yes, I hear you. I'll feed you, too."

Trey breathed a sigh of relief when she entered the kitchen with a smile on her face and a beaming Johnny cradled on one hip. She'd taken time to run a brush through her hair and clip back one side with a barrette. With blooming color back in her face, she was the antithesis of the ghost inhabiting her body the evening before.

Oh, Lareana, he thought, *if only you can hang on to your smile for the rest of the day.*

She did.

Until she saw Daniel Greaves in the court-room.

At the sight of the blue-clad man leaning nonchalantly back in his chair, visiting with his lawyer, the color drained from her face. When Greaves laughed at some remark, the cauldron inside her bubbled to a full boil once more.

Trey sensed the change immediately. So did her mother.

As the spectators settled themselves after the judge had been seated, Lareana glanced around the room. Both Brian Campbell and Cathy Hanson were there, along with a full contingent of reporters.

As the witnesses testified to the character of Daniel Greaves, his morality, his business credentials, Lareana remained frozen in place. She hardly appeared to breathe, but her darting eyes missed nothing.

When the counselor from the Alcohol Rehabilitation Center stated under oath that Mr. Greaves had responded well to treatment, her jaw locked in place.

They left for the luncheon recess, and a blatant headline from the newspaper stand across the hall grabbed their attention: " 'Hanging's Too Good for the Man!' Says Grieving Widow." A photo of Lareana leaving the building centered the page.

Trey waited for the explosion.

But Lareana clung stoically to her control.

Late in the afternoon, Daniel Greaves took the stand. His air of innocence endured until the prosecuting attorney began his barrage of questions. "I don't remember . . . I only had a couple of beers" became his litany. At no time did he even begin to acknowledge any responsibility.

Trey, watching carefully for any sign of response from Lareana, perceived the dilation of her eyes. One eyebrow lifted. *Hang on, love,* he thought. *Hang on.*

After the lawyer's closing remarks, the judge gave the jury their instructions, and the somber group filed from the room. The wait began.

Greaves rose, stretched, and shook hands with his attorney.

Lareana stood.

Greaves turned. He glanced around the room, casually, as if he hadn't a care in the world.

Lareana stared, waiting.

His eyes locked with hers for half a second, the blink of an eyelash. Then the contact severed. He moved on.

A wheelchair halfway blocked the door. Greaves brushed by without acknowledging the occupant.

The trial was over. Or was it?

Six

A door slammed in her mind.

As the corridor to reason closed, Lareana allowed Trey to lead her from the courtroom. With a slight nod, she acknowledged Brian Campbell and Cathy Hanson. Reporters hovered around them, breaking away to follow her and her family.

The late-afternoon sunshine was temporarily blinding as Trey and Lareana paused a moment on the top step of the courthouse. Flashbulbs added to the glare as they descended. Some of the crowd waved signs proclaiming: "Tougher Laws for Drunks," "Douse the Souses," and "Drinking and Driving Don't Mix."

Lareana ignored the reporters, brushing through the crowd as though it didn't exist. Her eyes were riveted on a male figure slouched against a late-model luxury car. Greaves finished lighting his cigarette and clicked the lighter shut.

The staccato beat of Lareana's high heels on the concrete sidewalk captured his attention. And everyone else's. She halted a couple of feet in front of him. Head high, honeyed hair tossed by the wind, her glacier eyes bored into his.

"I have a baby who will never see the father who loved him." Her voice carried clearly on the crisp air. "John is dead! You killed him! You and . . . your —" she strangled on the words — "couple of beers!"

The cauldron boiled over. The glacier melted in streams of tears as she turned into the circle of Trey's waiting arms. Trey waved the reporters away as he gently steered her toward the parking lot.

"Ah, Lareana," he murmured. "Cry it out, love. Cry it out."

"I hate him!" She hiccuped between words. "I hate him and all he stands for. He's not even in jail." She turned stark eyes on Trey. "What's to keep him from doing it again . . . drinking and d — driving that monstrous car of his?"

Trey shook his head. Nothing. He knew she didn't want to hear that answer. Nothing would happen unless a policeman picked him up again. Then Greaves would get another of his innumerable tickets. And maybe spend the night in the slammer, until his lawyer bailed him out again. No. It didn't seem fair to Trey either. He wiped a tear from her cheek with a compassionate forefinger.

"How long do you think the jury will be out?" Swen asked as they reached the cars. "Should we wait or go on home?"

Trey settled Lareana, wrapped securely in her mother's arms, into the back seat of his van. "You wait here and I'll go check."

Lareana felt like an empty reservoir, drained by the tempest of tears. Her eyes stung and her nose continued to drip. She blew into a handkerchief and burrowed closer to her mother's shoulder.

Trey rejoined the others. "It's so late today that we won't hear a verdict until tomorrow morning at the earliest. I asked someone to call us when the time comes."

"You'll call me as soon as you know anything, then?" Swen rubbed a work-worn hand through his thinning gray hair.

Trey nodded. "You won't come with us for dinner?"

"No. My cows need milking, trial or no trial." He reached inside the car to pat Lareana's shoulder and clasp his wife's hand. "You two take care now. I'll see you tomorrow."

Johnny took advantage of all the attention that evening. He found that tasty finger he'd enjoyed before, pulled at his grandmother's earrings, and tangled his fists in his mother's hair. Samson got slobbered on when he pushed an inquisitive nose near the baby's dimpled chin.

Lareana felt as if she was viewing the scene through binoculars, backwards. *Here is one life,* she thought, *and the trial today was another.* Traveling those miles in between was like going through a time warp.

After dinner, nursing Johnny in her chair before the crackling fire, she could hear Trey and her mother moving about the kitchen. Their soft conversation, with its indiscernible words, lent a soothing background music.

"I love her, you know," Trey was saying. "I have since the day I met her."

Margaret nodded. "We could tell."

"I haven't told her yet. I won't until she's ready."

"Six months isn't very long, you know . . . for grieving, that is." She hung up the dishtowel and sank into a chair by the table.

"I agree. But I've waited years for a

woman like her." The depth of his feelings reached out and assured Margaret's mothering heart.

"You've been divorced?"

"Yes."

"I hate to sound narrow, but the Bible and our church don't condone divorce."

"I don't, either. It wasn't my choice."

"Yes, Lareana told me." She stared down at the embroidered daisies on the light blue tablecloth. Before the silence became burdensome, she patted his hand, rose, and went into the other room. She turned back in the doorway. "Your bed is still here, if you'd like."

Well that wasn't so bad, Trey thought. *But I'll bet she doesn't change her mind easily.*

The call came early in the morning. The verdict would be announced at eleven. Lareana packed Johnny into his car carrier and swapped him into the back seat of Trey's silver and black van. Johnny's grandmother buckled herself in beside him.

"Sure is easier than that Corvette," Lareana whispered in the baby's ear before returning to her place in the front. The roomy interior offered sheer comfort.

Though the familiar flames flickered to life as they entered the chambers, Lareana doused them with buckets of cold reason. Screaming and hollering did no good. There had to be a better way. Trey kept a close eye on her as they found their places.

She held Johnny tightly as the foreman of the jury rose. He took a piece of paper to the judge and returned to his seat. In the quiet, she could have heard even a feather float to the floor.

The judge looked up. "Would the defendant please rise."

Daniel Greaves pushed himself to his feet. Gone were the nonchalant air, the doodling, and the whispered comments. One hand plucked at the knot in his tie. He forced himself to stand straight.

"The jury finds you . . . guilty as charged." The gavel slammed against the bench.

Lareana felt relief take the weight from her shoulders, giving her the freedom to smile up at Trey standing tall beside her. She squeezed Johnny close. The courtroom buzzed. Everyone seemed to breathe more easily.

Except for the ramrod-stiff man in front of the bench.

The judge rapped for order and glanced down at his calendar. "Sentencing will take place in two weeks."

That means it's still not over, Lareana

thought. *He'll still be free for another two weeks.* "What does it take to get someone like him locked away?" she asked no one in particular. "What's wrong with our laws?"

"I can answer that for you." Cathy Hanson had come up behind her. "People have to care enough to make tougher laws. We've been too lenient far too long."

Brian Campbell wheeled his chair up as she and Cathy entered the aisle. It made a good picture for the evening news — a woman with a baby in her arms and a man in a wheelchair.

Trey ran interference for them as they made their way to the car. He was never rude, but he clearly made his point. They had provided enough copy for the media.

"Thanks for being here with me." Lareana hugged both her father and mother. "You've been super." She gave her dad an extra hug and whispered in his ear, "Thanks for letting us have Mom the last couple of nights. I know it was lonely for you at home."

"You'll be all right now?" Swen grasped her shoulders.

"Yes." The confident ring was back in her voice. She waved Johnny's tiny fist in the air as the grandparents drove away.

"Do you have to rush away?" Lareana asked

when she and Trey returned to Three Trees Farm. "I thought maybe we could go for a walk or something."

Trey assumed his familiar pose, wrists draped across the steering wheel. He transferred his attention from the glorious sun making a last-ditch stand against the rains of winter to the woman beside him. Blue shadows under her eyes and a weary sag to her eyelids testified to the strain she'd been under. She looked as if she needed a long nap instead of a walk.

"If you'd like," was all he said. He rose from his seat and, bending nearly in half, walked to the rear seat of the van to unstrap the sleeping baby.

Lareana opened her door. Someone, somewhere, was burning leaves. The tang on the air drifted in. There was no mistaking the fragrance. A plaintive moo-o-o caught her ear. One of the cows had probably been left behind the herd as they grazed in the far pasture. Samson whined, front paws on the bottom step of the van. The snowy ruff around his neck needed a scratching.

Mt. Rainier guarded the end of the hay field and the man halfway down the fence line. Uncle Haakan was hard at work on the endless task of repairing the miles of fencing on the farm. In novels, this scene would be called pastoral, Lareana thought.

A weary smile kissed the corners of her mouth. *Thank you, God, for these surroundings to come home to.* She inhaled a deep breath, expelling the last vestiges of the courtroom and breathing in the peace of home.

Trey watched the transformation in silence. With the baby carrier in his arms, he had no hands to help her down. But now she didn't need that support. He was glad and sad at the same time. Like everyone everywhere, he needed to be needed.

A companionable silence surrounded them as they reached the apple orchard a short time later. Johnny had gone back to sleep in the backpack strapped to Trey's shoulders. Lareana chose two perfect, blush-kissed King apples and tossed one to Trey. One crisp bite, and she had to wipe the juice from her chin. He shared her grin as he wiped the remaining drip from the side of her smile. The urge to kiss it away prolonged the silence.

Lareana felt breathless, as if all the world was waiting in the wings for the next move. She stared into the depths of the azure eyes above her. Trey bent his head; she raised hers. That fraction of space remained until the sweetness of their breaths mingled, drawing lips and hearts into mutual surrender. Her lashes fluttered closed as his warm mouth covered hers, tentatively at first, then securely when his hands rose to grasp her shoulders.

Trey raised his head just enough to give them breathing time. "You taste like apple and honey and all things sweet," he whispered.

"The apple is understandable." The sparkle had returned to her eyes. She stood on tiptoe to return the offering and gave him three feather-soft kisses, one on each corner of his chiseled lips and one in the middle, prolonging the moment. "But when finding honey, beware the bee sting." She gently nipped his bottom lip.

Trey's chuckle was buried in the strands of tousled gold as he wrapped both arms around her and hugged her close. She fit just right against his heart and under his chin. Would that she could stay there forever.

They followed the cow path down the fence line to where Uncle Haakan stretched barbed wire, pounding staples to secure it to a newly replaced cedar post.

Lareana detailed the happenings of the trial while Haakan pounded away. His nods served as vocabulary until he noticed baby Johnny stretching and yawning.

"Good day to you, too, youngstuff," he said, a calloused forefinger caressing the baby's cheek. Johnny grinned, his new tooth gleaming in the sunlight. Arms and legs flailing, he reached for the old man's finger, ready to chew away. Haakan chuckled and turned back to his fencing.

"Nice to see you again, Trey." He paused between one staple and another. "Those apples good this year?" He winked at Lareana and resumed his labors.

Lareana thumped him lovingly on the arm as her peals of laughter answered his dig.

That sly old fox, Trey thought. *Doesn't miss a thing, does he? Wonder if that meant approval? Sounded like it to me.* Trey caught Lareana's sidelong glance, smothered in mirth, as they continued down the cow path to the woods.

A deep drainage ditch traversed the field in front of the line of Juneberry bushes and wild rose canes. Bright red rose hips made the bushes a banquet table for the birds Trey and Lareana heard calling to each other. They followed the rim of the ditch back to a culvert in the road. Crossing over, Trey glanced up at the sky in time to see a hawk wheeling above the tall firs in the background. His screech floated down to them, one more note in a perfect symphony.

They traversed the rutted road among the alder saplings and scrub brush and stopped at the edge of another large hay field, this one bounded by second-growth timber of fir and alder. "This is one of my favorite places to ride."

"Beside the creek."

She nodded as she scuffed one booted toe in the grass. Then, hands in her back jeans pockets, she raised her face to the sun. "We'll go again if my new slave driver of a boss gives me any time."

Trey smiled as he snuggled her in his arms. "The other day I was a knight in a shiny Corvette, today I'm a slave driver. Make up thy mind, woman."

Lareana slipped her arm around his waist as they turned and started back up the road. "We can go by and see the horses if you like. They're pastured on the other side of the milking parlor." She tried to adjust her stride to his longer one. "Next time we'll go riding up on the logging roads into the Bald Hills."

Later that evening, after Trey had left and Johnny was fast sleep, Lareana finally allowed the morning's drama a place in her thoughts. *There must be something I can do,* she thought as she climbed the stairs to bed, *some way to publicize the need for tougher laws to protect people against drunk drivers. Funny, you never pay attention to things like this until you're caught right in the middle.*

And in the middle was where she found herself the next morning when she answered the phone.

"Appear on TV?" Her strangled gasp adequately communicated her shock. "You've got to be kidding!"

The voice on the other end assured her such was not the case. "And it would be a help if you brought your baby. It should be a simple interview. Because of the Daniel Greaves trial, we're doing a week-long series on the effects of drunk driving. I know you're concerned about this problem."

"But . . . but —" Lareana thought back to the night before. *I didn't pray for this, did I?* She took a deep breath, feeling like a diver about to leap . . . into a teacup.

"Of . . . of course. What do you want me to do?" she asked finally. After the conversation, it took a supreme act of will to remove her permanently clamped fingers from the phone.

Trey thought it was great. "You've got a story to tell. Go for it."

Easy for him to say, Lareana thought. *He's not doing the interview.*

In three days Lareana found herself and Johnny standing just off the set, waiting for their turn in front of the camera. Trey had an important business meeting scheduled, but he had promised to tape the television show on his VCR. Then he and Lareana could watch it together. Her parents and aunt and uncle were parked in front of their sets at home.

Black hair and snapping dark eyes proclaimed the Hispanic heritage of the woman approaching her charges. With spritely grace, Juanita Evans crossed the cable-strewn floor, all the while chatting sociably to put Lareana at ease.

It didn't help much, even though she was already getting to be an old hand at this TV stuff. Juanita and her crew had been out at the farm the day before, taping scenes of Lareana and Johnny at home on the farm. The news team was trying to include a real human-interest angle without being morbid. The grin on Johnny's face as he waved and slobbered definitely wasn't morbid.

When they taped those first scenes, Lareana had been on her home turf. The camera had worked around her and her daily schedule. An interview on set was a completely different story, or so the butterflies and all their cousins cavorting in her midsection informed her.

"Can I get you anything?" Juanita asked. She seated Lareana and Johnny on a sofa. When the floor director clipped a microphone to the lapel of Lareana's indigo blazer, Johnny's chubby fingers zeroed in like a hawk diving for prey.

Lareana disengaged his fist and dug into his diaper bag for one of his favorite toys. She waved the bright red ring enticingly in front of him, but there was no thrill like a new thrill for the inquisitive baby. Back to the mike. Lareana's finger became the pacifier as Johnny guided it to his mouth and proceeded to chew. He paid no attention to the cameras, but smiles creased the faces of the circumspect crew. He took the finger out of his mouth, studied it carefully, jabbered and drooled, and stuck it back in again. Lareana was concentrating so hard on keeping her son occupied she had no idea what a picture they made.

A still frame of John and one of their wedding flashed on the screen, after the segments from the farm. Lareana's honesty in answering the questions revealed not only her own feelings but the universal feelings of drunk-driving victims everywhere.

"I'm having a hard time looking at alcohol dependency as a disease right now," she said. "And it's almost impossible not to hate the man who caused John's death. It might have been different if this had been Greaves' first offense —" she paused, glanced at Juanita, and continued — "but then again, maybe not."

"What do you see as necessary changes?"

"Tighter laws. If people were afraid of heavy fines and automatic jail sentences, maybe they would slow down their drinking, or at least not drive when they've been drinking alcohol. It seems drinkers can't tell they've had too many until it's too late."

"And now the phone lines are open for your calls." Juanita turned toward the camera and smiled. "Hello, you're on News at Noon."

A male voice came over the wire. "My wife was killed by a drunk driver —" When he went on, the huskiness in his voice had deepened. "Now I'm raising three children by myself. I agree with you. Sometimes it's hard not to hate. I can't get dependable help. What do you say to toddlers when Mommy doesn't come home? It's tearing me up —" His voice broke.

"Thank you for calling." Juanita's tone

was like the kiss of caring.

Lareana felt tears burning behind her eyelids. She blinked rapidly, using Johnny's blond head as a shield. The remaining calls were similar. All were stories of tragedy, shattered lives, and broken people.

"Our guest tomorrow will be Brian Campbell, another victim whose life was changed by drunk-driving." Juanita closed, "Thank you for watching News at Noon."

After the floor director completed the countdown, Juanita turned to Lareana. "You were wonderful. How do you feel?"

"The time zipped by. I have so many more things I'd like to say."

"Well, thank you again. And —" Juanita's voice softened — "I know what it's like to be on the other side of the fence. My father was an alcoholic. I lived in mortal fear that he would injure someone else or himself. Thank God, he always made it home in one piece, car and all."

"What finally happened?"

"He went to Alcoholics Anonymous. Hasn't had a drink in ten years."

Lareana squeezed the woman's hand. "Your story has a happy ending. Maybe you need to share that kind of result in your special reports."

When Lareana and Johnny got out to the

149

car, she started to strap in his seat, but his nuzzling mouth told her what he wanted. Food. Making herself comfortable, she flipped the blanket over her shoulder. "At least your fast-food chain is portable. Wonder what we could call it. Mom's? Milk on Demand?" She smoothed the downy cheek snuggled against her breast. "Oh, Johnny boy, I love you."

When his long lashes fluttered closed and stayed there, she put him back in his seat and headed for home.

When Trey arrived that evening, he grabbed her and spun her around. "You were wonderful! Here —" He plugged in his VCR and slipped in the cassette. Instantly, Lareana and Johnny, slobber and all, appeared on the television screen in full color.

When the program was over, Lareana leaned back in her chair and turned to look at Trey. He was sitting with elbows on his knees, hands folded, steeple-like, under his chin.

"I heard of a new organization today." He tapped his two index fingers together.

"Oh?"

"It's called CORD — Citizens Organized for Responsible Drinking. Some of the restaurant owners were talking about it."

He rubbed his hands together slowly. "You might consider getting involved in it."

"Are you going to?"

"I'm thinking about it. It might be a place to start lobbying. The legislature is where laws are changed."

"I think I'd better start at the library." Lareana switched off the TV set. "I don't really know much about all this — the laws, the proposed changes, or even what works in other places."

The phone rang. Lareana's eyebrows arched toward her hairline.

"Not the first, huh?" Trey locked his fingers behind his head, spreading wide the lapels of his gray silk suit jacket. As usual, he looked as if he had written and produced an ad for menswear, then starred in it.

"Nope. Guess this makes me a celebrity." Her grin deepened the dimples in her cheeks. "But the real one is sound asleep in there."

She answered the phone and came back. "You should have heard his grandma. Grandpa, too. They couldn't stop talking long enough for me to get a word in edgewise. Ah, well, I'll enjoy it while it lasts."

"You wouldn't by any chance have a cup of coffee or something out there, would you?"

"If by 'something' you're referring to goodies, you're in trouble. But I have coffee or herb tea, if you prefer."

He rotated his head, seeking to release the tension in his shoulders. "Tea sounds fine."

"If you'll sit in here where I can reach you, I'll rub your neck for you while I'm making the tea."

"That's a deal no one would pass up." He rose to his feet. Removing his jacket, he folded it carefully over the back of a chair.

Lareana had the teakettle on the stove and the mugs down before Trey entered the kitchen. When he sat in the straight-backed chair, she began her ministrations. Her hands, accustomed to hard work, were strong, and she knew how to pinch, press, and pummel each muscle and tendon into submission.

Trey let his head drop forward, the relaxation permeating deep into his neck and shoulders. When the teakettle shrieked, he jerked, aware that he'd almost fallen asleep.

He smiled at her over the steaming mug. "You're a woman of many talents." He inhaled deeply. "What is this?"

"My own special blend. They say that if you like the aroma, you'll love the flavor. I like honey with mine." She set a hand-thrown honey jar in front of him. A tiny clay bear straddled the lid.

"I suppose you made the honey, too?" He twirled the wooden dipstick around and held it over his cup. The golden syrup flowed into a thread-thin stream.

"Uncle Haakan did. Or rather his bees did. That's one of his hobbies. Sure helps our orchards out, too."

He sipped from the rim of his delft blue mug. "This is good . . . really good. "You people are remarkable. Are there any of the old crafts you don't do?"

Lareana appeared to ponder his question. "I'll tell you a secret . . . that is, if you promise not to divulge it to the world."

"Trust me. I have my Agent 0010 badge from my Toastie Flakes box. That makes me irreproachable." He leaned forward, one hand cupped behind his ear.

Lareana lowered her voice to a conspiratorial whisper. "I don't make soap."

"I'm crushed." He clutched one hand to the general region of his heart, and waved the other hand, barker-like. "I had planned on a Super Soap Service at Timber Country. All homemade. Gentle enough to soothe the complexions of the fairest of the fair damsels. By the way, were there damsels in the lumber camps?"

"I think all the damsels stayed in Europe.

Along with the knights in shining armor. Or so they say."

He set his mug down with a thump. "Have I told you about the meeting next week? The one with the think tank executives from Six Flags and Magic Mountain?"

Lareana shook her head.

"I want you to be in on it, at least while we're discussing plans for the restaurant." He rose and went back into the living room to retrieve his jacket. Removing the calendar from an inner pocket, he checked the dates. "We should be covering that part of the planning by Wednesday. Could you come for the day?"

"I — I suppose so." She mentally counted off the days. "Will you be free for the sentencing?"

"No, but I'll be there anyway." He checked his calendar again. "If you want to bring Johnny and stay overnight at my condominium the day of the Timber Country meeting, it might make it easier for you. My housekeeper, Ada, would love to watch him for the day, while we're in the meetings."

Trey watched for her response. *Almost blew that,* he thought. *Please don't misunderstand, Lareana.*

Lareana stared over the rim of her mug at the man sitting across from her. He made it all sound so simple. Just come up there. No problem. She'd have to wean that son of hers pretty soon.

She shook her head. "I'll come for the day. But that's all. Saturday Aunt Inga and I are having a recipe test day with the antique recipes I've collected so far."

"Sounds great. Wish I could come taste." He shrugged into his jacket. "I've got to get going. I'll call you tomorrow."

Lareana rose and stepped into his arms like a homing pigeon come to roost. The warm pressure of his lips on hers elicited a soft sigh, a whisper of surrender, the breath of love.

But Lareana didn't know it yet.

SEVEN

"Who can that be?"

Samson's barking had reached a piercing pitch by the time Lareana opened the door. A clown, wearing a red costume with white polka dots on one side and the reverse on the other, tipped his fireman's hat, honked a horn tied to his belt, and handed her an armful of stuffed bears. The bear's T-shirt barely covered a rounded tummy.

"Pooh Bear?" She looked back at the clown. He nodded — vigorously. He touched his head with one finger as if he'd just remembered, and drew a card from a huge pocket sewn on one pants leg. With a flourish, he presented the card to her.

Samson growled in the background.

Already laughing at the clown's antics, Lareana maneuvered around the bear to open the card. "A honey jar always needs a Pooh Bear. Trey."

Lareana wasn't sure if the tears in her eyes

were from laughter or — She extended her hand. The clown c-a-r-e-f-u-l-l-y wiped his hand on his suit, both down the leg and across the chest, then gave her hand a single shake. He tooted his horn and leaped off the stairs, clicking his heels on the way.

Hugging Pooh Bear to her chest, Lareana stood in the doorway until the rainbow-hued van drove out of sight.

The man's crazy, she thought. *And how I love it!* Something stirred just on the edges of her subconsciousness. She paused, waiting for it to come nearer. It was something good, she could tell. But what? When nothing further materialized, she went about her day, mentally ticking off her tasks. She'd start with a phone call to a certain business-man in Seattle.

Trey was out of the office. "Would you please give him this message?" Lareana asked. " 'Pooh's stuck in the honey again. Now what?' "

A brief silence preceded the secretary's strangled, "Of course."

The next morning found Lareana up to her elbows in cornmeal, flour, and more apples. She carefully read the brief instructions for scrapple, a breakfast staple in the old logging camps. "Mix sausage with cornmeal

mush and let set overnight. Slice and fry."
Should she fry the sausage first? What did
one put the dough — the mess — in to set?
How much cornmeal? As in the past, she
waited for Aunt Inga. All her years of cooking school, and she had never learned to
make scrapple. She grinned inwardly.

Maybe she'd have better luck with apple
pan dowdy. She reread the recipe. And then
again, maybe not.

When Inga arrived, the two women attacked the matter at hand. Step one: Decipher the recipes.

By the time several hours had passed, the
results of their labors lined the counters.
The scrapple filled a bread pan in the
refrigerator, ready to slice and fry, then
serve with syrup. Lareana had decided her
apple crisp recipe was far superior to apple
pan dowdy.

"I agree," Aunt Inga said as she relaxed at
the table with a cup of Lareana's herb tea.
"We ought to try cornmeal griddlecakes one
of these times. As I remember, they were
really good. Filling, too."

"I've tried buckwheat pancakes before."
Lareana sipped her tea while she wrote in
her comments on the recipes. She kept a
record of all her experiments — both the
successes and the failures — in a blue

158

notebook. "But I think sourdough pancakes will be our hottest seller. I talked with one of the menu-planners for a chain of pancake houses. We agreed that the restaurant should offer several kinds. One of those diaries I found said the logging cooks varied the kinds of flapjacks, but didn't have more than one kind on any one day."

"It's the toppings that will sell. Your blackberry syrup beats anything I've tasted." Inga glanced toward the kettle bubbling gently on the stove. "And that hot apple compote . . . my, my."

Lareana flashed a grin at the compliment as she continued to write. "It's not as if I came up with that one myself. Seems to me you had a hand in it. You and your 'pinch of this' and 'touch of that.' Hard to measure those amounts."

"Lareana?"

The golden-haired young woman raised her head at the question in her aunt's voice. "What?"

"You've been seeing a mighty lot of that young man lately, haven't you?"

Lareana nodded.

"You know we want nothing but your happiness." Inga reached over and patted her niece's hand.

She nodded again and waited.

"It's just that John hasn't been gone too long. We wouldn't want you to be hurt or . . . well . . . for people to talk."

Lareana could tell it was hard for her aunt to give unsolicited advice. "Don't worry." She turned her hand and squeezed Inga's gnarled fingers. "He's just a friend. A good friend."

Sunday morning arrived along with a rainstorm that didn't slow Trey down. He wheeled the van around the drive in plenty of time to take Lareana and Johnny to church. When she opened the door, he brushed her lips in a brief hello.

This could get to be a habit, she thought as she inhaled the scent of his aftershave. Before she could react, he had picked up the baby carrier and packed it out to the van, all the while exchanging absurdities with the bouncy baby.

"Would Haakan and Inga like to ride with us?" he asked as he strapped the carrier into place.

"They're almost ready." She slid the diaper bag in next to the seat. As Trey settled her in the front seat and shut the van door, she had the strongest urge to reach over and kiss him again. Definitely habit-forming.

On the ride to the little country church, Trey charmed Haakan and Inga with stories of hay ranching in George. When they entered the front door, the crowd began to buzz about their local television stars, and Johnny was passed around and cooed over.

Their interest in Trey came more in the form of sidelong glances from the women, handshakes from the men, and snickers from the teen-age girls. He was a real eye-catcher in a navy suede blazer and gray wool slacks. Light caught the raindrops in his hair and sparkled sienna. Her eyes were drawn to the laughter beaming from his eyes and then to his mouth, curved in an engaging smile, asking to be kissed. So much for objectivity.

In the sanctuary, the organist was playing a medley of Lareana's favorite hymns. A hush descended over the congregation as the pastor bowed his head before the altar and began the service. When Johnny fell promptly asleep, Lareana found her attention drifting to the man beside her. She'd jerk it back to the order of service, only to find it roaming again. She'd forgotten the simple pleasures of tall shoulders next to her own, a masculine hand helping to hold the hymnal, a deep baritone voice belting out the hymns. And again the scent of his aftershave drifted by her.

Pastor Jensguard emphasized the words of the Scripture: "Beloved, let us love one another, for love is of God —"

The words leaped out at Lareana. That's what had been at the rim of her consciousness. She didn't just love Trey as a brother or a fellow human being. She was in love with him. And this kind of love was also from God. Trey had come into her life so unexpectedly, but just when she needed him. And yesterday she'd told Inga he was "just" a friend. Hmm-m-m.

Suddenly Trey sensed a new air of wonder in her. He'd been intensely aware of her from the moment he arrived at the farm. The winter rose tone of her wool crepe dress brought out the bloom in her cheeks and complemented the clarity of her complexion. Tendrils of goldenrod hair called to his fingers. Her slightly gathered skirt whispered against her when she crossed her legs. The haunting fragrance of her perfume drifted unseen, but never unsensed, around her, summoning . . . no . . . demanding, his attention. Sitting next to her was joy, was agony, was where he always wanted to be.

They stood for the closing hymn.

Back in the van, Lareana was delighted when Haakan and Inga accepted Trey's invitation to dinner. Wasn't she? The desire to tell Trey of her new discovery warred with the knowledge that he'd never said he loved her. Or had he? Wasn't he showing it by all he did? Her mind flitted back to their conversations. What had he called her? "Lareana, love"? Did it mean what she thought, or was it just a nickname?

She refused to replay those "love me, love me not" games of her teen years. Her internal instructions were adamant. She would discuss her knowledge with Trey that day. A thrill of anticipation tuned every sense to concert pitch.

Dinner at the Oyster House in Olympia met that restaurant's usual good standards. It wasn't their fault that Lareana thought the service was slow.

And Haakan and Inga were just being their normally gracious selves when they invited her and Trey in for coffee and dessert. Weren't they?

Now I'll get Johnny down for a long nap so we can talk, she thought as they finally arrived at her own door. But Johnny had been napping already. Instead, he woke up . . . screaming. When she changed his diaper, the heat from his restless body nearly burned her fingers.

She tested his temperature. The look on

her face warned Trey there was trouble.

"It's 104°," she said softly.

"You're calling the doctor?" When she nodded, Trey picked up the crying baby. "I'll hold him."

"I'll meet you at my office in fifteen minutes," Dr. Pat's calm voice reassured Lareana's racing fears. "It's probably an ear infection if it came on that fast. You say he hasn't been sick until now?"

"Just drooling and a runny nose once in a while. I figured it was from teething."

"That'll do it. See you as soon as you can get there."

It was, as Dr. Pat had suspected, a simple ear infection. But someone forgot to tell Johnny about "simple." He cried and fussed in their arms. Even laying him down caused a knee-jerk reaction. He'd start to doze off, then cry again, until finally the drops began to take effect.

Trey hated to leave, but he had to be at his office early in the morning. He waited until the baby's cries had turned to whimpers. Lareana walked with him to the door, Johnny snuggled against her shoulder.

"I'll call you in the morning," Trey whispered, dropping a kiss on each of their foreheads. He started down the stairs, then turned. "Are you sure you'll be all right?"

Lareana nodded. "Dr. Pat said twenty-four hours. You heard her." *So much for telling him my feelings,* she thought. All her lovely dreams . . . well, babies came first.

He slipped a hand beneath the hair on her neck and brought her lips to his.

Johnny moaned again, one tiny fist clutching the collar of her blouse.

Trey saluted with three fingers to his forehead and left.

Dr. Pat was right. By the next morning Johnny was feeling much better. Lareana, however, felt as if she'd been up most of the night, which she had. So she decided to take a nap when the baby did.

Even though she was worn out, thoughts of Greaves intruded on her rest. The anger hadn't died, it was only banked. She shut her eyes again. She'd deal with that later. She just as resolutely pushed away any thoughts about forgiveness. The ringing of the telephone brought her back from a lovely dream. There had been sunshine, birds singing, and she and Trey, alone on the grass beneath a tree. When she heard his voice on the phone, it was as if the dream continued.

"Good morning, love. How's the patient?"

"He's better."

"Did I wake you?"

"Um-m-mm." Lareana stretched both arms above her head, the phone clamped on one shoulder. She twisted, reveling in the almost sinful treat of waking halfway through the morning. "But that's all right."

"Has he been there yet?"

Lareana was instantly awake, the dream banished. "Who?"

"If you have to ask, he hasn't."

"Trey, what are you talking about?" A low laugh came through the wire. "Trey!"

"Enjoy your day, lady fair. I'm off to slay dragons." The dial tone filled her ear.

Lareana shook her head. Crazy man.

Shortly after noon, Lareana found out who "he" was. Samson heralded the arrival of Dan's Deliveries, a van painted bright red with a sign in iridescent letters: "We deliver anything . . . anywhere." The "anything" a cheery young man pulled from the back doors would please any little boy's heart. A toddler's rocking horse, more like a rocking cart, complete with seat belt, came first. The red and white painted pony sported a card that read, "To my second favorite TV star. Rock on."

The miniature red cowboy hat was trimmed with white as were the chaps and vest. The hat on the cuddly teddy bear matched. "You gotta dress for the part," read that card.

Fits of hilarity attacked both Lareana and the delivery man as they carried the booty to the house.

"That must be some proud daddy," he said. "I've never seen such a layout."

Lareana never bothered to correct him.

"Trey is out of the office," his secretary intoned.

"Tell him 'Hi, ho, Old Paint, and away.' " Lareana had a hard time keeping a straight face.

"R — Right," the woman stammered, her tone questioning.

On Wednesday morning, Lareana dressed in her most businesslike attire. She needed all the confidence she could dig up before the meeting. Whenever she thought about it, her resident troupe of butterflies turned handsprings.

She started out with her navy suit, but remembering Trey had seen that, she switched to gray. The soft, untailored jacket topped a silk turquoise blouse and a loosely pleated skirt. She loved the casually elegant feeling the outfit gave her. Silver chains and hoop earrings, suede pumps, and matching purse tied everything together. She swept her hair back into a French twist with her bangs brushed to one side. She stared at herself in the full-length mirror.

"Not bad." She added a little extra teal eyeshadow. "Not bad at all." She had already taken Johnny over to Inga's. With Lareana gone so much, the older couple had hired the extra help the farm needed. Uncle Haakan could never have kept it all up by himself.

But it would be this way more and more. As she drove out the leaf-encrusted drive, she thought, *I'm becoming a businesswoman now.*

She held on to that thought two hours later as she parked in a garage in downtown Seattle. The ride to the tenth floor gave her no time to adjust to city speed before she entered the Surf and Turf executive offices.

"Mrs. Amundson? I'm Sandy." An energetic young woman rose from behind the reception desk. At Lareana's nod, she continued, "Mr. Bennett said to bring you to the board room as soon as you arrived." She started to lead the way down the hall. "Can I get you anything before we go?"

"No, thank you." Lareana controlled the tremor in her voice.

Following the receptionist down the hall

gave Lareana time to glance at the textured oil paintings of the Northwest lining the walls. Pictures of Surf and Turf restaurants surrounded a sign boasting "Timber Country" in carved wooden letters on the end wall.

"Here we are." Sandy opened a solid oak door and motioned Lareana to precede her.

The board room looked as if it had just been lifted out of a business magazine. High-backed, leather-padded chairs surrounded a long oak table. To Lareana, it looked long enough to seat a football team and their families for Thanksgiving dinner. At the far end, picture windows overlooked Puget Sound, gray today like the clouds overhead.

Lareana took a deep breath and raised her chin a bit higher than normal. Her smile securely in place, she crossed to the head of the table.

The meeting was already in session, but Trey rose immediately at Sandy's touch on his arm. His eyes lit up at the sight of Lareana.

"We'll take a break now." He motioned to the group and took Lareana by the arm. "How's Youngstuff doing? Any trouble on the way up? How's the farm? It's so good to see you." He stopped talking to stare at her, longing to take her in his arms.

"Fine, no, great, and I agree."

Trey looked at her, dumbfounded.

"I was just answering your questions. You didn't give me a moment."

Trey threw back his head, his laughter drawing the attention of the people around the coffee cart. "Come on, fair lady, let's go meet the experts."

Soon her mind was a muddle of names and faces. The one person who stood out was Mrs. Quinelli, Trey's secretary. Lareana smiled at the expression on the dignified woman's face and extended her hand. "I'm glad to meet you — especially after the messages you've been passing on for me."

"Excuse me for a moment," Trey said. He flagged down one of the board members, leaving the two women to get acquainted.

"My dear, you've certainly touched his life in a special way." Mrs. Quinelli nodded toward the man who stood half a head above the others. She squeezed Lareana's hand once more. "Can I get you something? Coffee, rolls? We have about anything you could want over there."

"Thanks. I'll see." The two of them made their way through the group. Trey was calling the meeting back to order, so Lareana took a glass of orange juice and sat beside him as he gestured for her to do. Mrs. Quinelli was on her other side, carefully recording the proceedings.

"Feel free to join the discussions any time," Trey spoke into Lareana's ear as he took his place beside her again. His hand had brushed her shoulder as he pushed her chair in.

Lareana smiled her thanks.

The hours until noon melted away faster than snowflakes on an upturned cheek. Lareana listened carefully while she studied the charts and diagrams posted around the room. Possible layouts covered one portable easel, and schematics of existing theme parks were tacked on another. An artist had been commissioned to paint a watercolor of the entrance to the park. Two bark-covered logs held up a third, with "Timber Country" carved in bas-relief. It looked tall enough for Paul Bunyan to walk under.

At the word *restaurant,* Lareana's full attention snapped back to the discussion. As they referred to "the restaurant" time after time, Lareana cleared her throat. "I'd like to suggest a name."

Trey nodded at her. "Go ahead."

"Why not just the 'Cookhouse' or 'Cookshack'? That's what they called the dining areas back then."

Trey pondered for a moment. "Why not 'Swen's Cookhouse'? We have 'Ole's Barn' for the animals."

Lareana beamed her appreciation at his use of her father's name. "And the outside should be rustic, with vertical rough-sawn boards and a shake roof. A wooden porch with a slanted roof could extend along the front. No matter how large your building is, it would look authentic."

She laid a picture from an antique book on logging camps on the table before them. Her description was indeed accurate.

Trey nodded to the architects, halfway down the table. "You got that?"

At that point, others chimed in with ideas, both for the cookshack and other eating establishments on the grounds. Swen's Cookhouse, however, would be the only one with a sit-down dining room.

"Will the saloon be in the same building, or in a separate one?" asked one of the architects.

"You might want to have both," someone else added. "A lounge at the cookshack and then a separate building with a false front and swinging doors for the saloon."

"You're right on target," Trey responded.

Lareana felt as if she'd been run over by a two-ton bull. With each word, she felt hooves pounding her into the ground.

No, Trey, you can't do this! She wanted to shake him. Waiting for the confrontation, she retreated to the depths of her chair.

Sensing her stillness, Trey dismissed everyone for lunch, inviting them to gather in the room down the hall. The meal would be served immediately. As they all filed from the room, still discussing the plans, Trey turned to Lareana.

"Okay, what's the problem?" His direct attack brought her eyes up to meet his.

"What do you mean, *saloon?*" She tried to keep her voice steady. "I thought we agreed that this was to be a family park."

"It is. What we agreed to was to disagree until I could do some more research."

"I thought that, since we hadn't discussed it anymore, you'd changed your mind."

Trey crossed his arms over his chest and slouched on the arm of the chair next to her.

She was adamant. "Is it really so necessary to offer liquor?"

"Lareana, you know from your chef's training that most of the money made in a restaurant is from the bar. Good food and good service are imperative, but it's the bar that makes the profit."

"It doesn't have to."

173

"No, it doesn't. But you know my restaurants have a good reputation. My bartenders are trained in all the latest techniques for discouraging drunk driving. This wouldn't be any different."

Lareana chewed on her bottom lip, one finger rubbing the back of another. She didn't want to be involved in a place that served drinks. She just couldn't. What if a drunk left the park and murdered someone else? Someone with a family? Wouldn't that make her an accomplice?

But she did want to help build this park, create a fun place for people to enjoy themselves. She sighed. She was beginning to sound like Trey.

Trey watched the emotions play tag across her face. *Come on, Lareana. We can work something out.* He wanted to reach over and take her in his arms. Instead, he waited. "Can we again agree to disagree for the time being?" he asked. "And go eat? They'll all be finished before we get started."

Lareana stared at him, her eyes dark with indecision. With a barely perceptible nod, she rose to her feet.

The rest of the day wasn't much of an improvement over the first part. Lareana contributed her ideas, and everyone was quick to agree that lumberjack breakfasts served all day would be a unique feature. They liked the thought, too, of wooden covered wagons with one side raised for serving soft drinks, cider, and apple pizza. Trey promised them all free samples at their next meeting.

But her participation didn't help to ease her own apprehension. She just couldn't get the thought of the saloon out of her mind.

When Trey dismissed the group for the day, Lareana rose and went to stand in front of the windows. The low-hanging clouds were spilling their despair in drifting sheets of rain over Seattle and the Sound. Lareana felt like joining them.

After finishing his discussion with a member of the think tank, Trey came to stand behind her. He circled her waist with his arms and drew her back against the length of his body.

With a sigh, she leaned against the solid wall of his chest and closed her eyes. His warm breath stirred the feathery wisps of her bangs as he touched his lips to her temple, once and then again. She covered his clasped hands with her own and offered up another sigh, this one from her feelings of discouragement, frustration, resentment. She wasn't sure which.

"Do you want to talk about it?" His question came softly against her skin.

Did she? She wasn't sure. Maybe discussing it would help them reach a compromise, but then again, was a compromise possible? All she knew was that she didn't want to make any decisions right now. She shook her head. "Just hold me."

Trey knew he'd have no trouble with that suggestion. They watched the lights dress up the curve of the waterfront. Headlights flashed, bumper to bumper, on Alaskan Way below them, but they were high above the clamor of the rush-hour traffic. The only sound in the paneled room was their steady breathing — unless one considered the thudding of their hearts worthy of mention.

Trey thought back over their conversation about liquor in restaurants. As a decision tightened his jaw, he turned her around to face him. "Lareana, I have to show you something. It won't take a great deal of time, and it's right on your way home."

"What is it?"

"I'll show you." He took her arm, handed her her purse as they passed the chair, and marched her out the door.

"Trey!" Lareana pulled back. "I've got to get home. Johnny will be needing me."

"As I said, this won't take long."

Once in the elevator, Trey leaned back

against the wall, allowing the weariness of a week of day and night meetings to seep through him. The plans were going well, but he'd found his energy divided, part of him wanting to be with Lareana. He slipped an arm around her waist and drew her to him. "Have I told you today how lovely you look?"

"No, but thanks, and I agree." She grinned. "That is . . . you do, too." Glad for the change of topic, she tapped him lightly on the navy and crimson silk tie he still had knotted loosely around his neck. She reached up and softly brushed his lips with hers.

Trey gathered her closer. This was surely what he needed after a long day — this woman not only in his dreams but in his arms.

"Where are we going?" Lareana asked against his lips as the elevator door opened.

"It's not far. You can follow me in your car."

"Trey —" The insistence in her tone was wasted on her escort. He merely continued to his own car.

A few minutes later, they pulled into the parking lot of the downtown Surf and Turf. Their difficulty in finding a parking place only proved the popularity of the establishment.

Trey led her into the lounge.

As her eyes adjusted to the dimness, Lareana looked around with interest. A carved antique bar with a cut-glass mirror behind it dominated one end of the room. Comfortable padded chairs circled small round tables. While most of them were full, the sound of conversation was only a low rumble. Waitresses, dressed in long burgundy skirts and tailored white blouses, added another touch of elegance.

Trey stopped at the bar and waited for the busy man behind it to have a free moment. "Lareana Amundson, I'd like you to meet Ted Crofton. He's been with me since this place opened." Lareana extended her hand, and it was engulfed by the large paw of the beaming, bald-headed man.

"I'm pleased to meet you." Ted's deep and powerful voice matched his body. "Can I get you something?"

Lareana glanced at Trey. "A diet cola would be fine . . . if you have it?"

"Ted, I'd like you to show Lareana the things we do here to encourage safe driving. Is there someone who can take over for you for a few minutes?"

After Ted called over one of the waitresses

to fill his job and poured the diet drink, he turned to Lareana. "You knew, of course, that Trey is the president of a group of restaurant owners organized to promote safe driving?"

Lareana shook her head. *I wonder what else I don't know about this man,* she thought.

"And I suppose he's told you about the equipment we've installed, the breathalyzer, the —"

"No." She glanced up at Trey.

"That's what I want *you* to do," Trey said. "I have a phone call to make. Be right back."

"Come right this way, Ms. Amundson." Ted smiled at her.

In the following minutes, Lareana received a complete lesson in the state-of-the-art techniques the restaurant employed. She learned how the breathalyzer worked, how quickly alcohol moved into one's system, and some of the tricks people used to try to fool themselves and the machines. A sign above the counter read: "The management reserves the right to call a taxi for anyone deemed too inebriated to drive." The bartenders also refused service to patrons at their discretion.

"Do you find that some still get by you?" Lareana was quick to ask.

"Sometimes," Ted nodded. "But we tell

the waitresses to keep track of how many drinks a patron has had, then the breathalyzer is used. And we're all pretty good judges of people by now. Besides, we've been known to call the cops when someone refuses to comply." He nodded wisely. "Word gets around."

"Hasn't it hurt your business?"

"Surprisingly, not much. If someone deliberately goes over his limit, the cabbies will cooperate. Trey has his parking lots patrolled, so if a car is left here, it's safe. As I said, word gets around."

Lareana glanced toward the corner as a ripple of guitar chords announced the evening's entertainment. A young woman with cascading midnight hair perched on a tall stool and adjusted the microphones. Her voice was mellow and haunting as she broke into the opening bars of a well-known love song.

Lareana listened for a moment. For a change, the volume wasn't turned up to deafening proportions.

Her attention was caught by a man about to leave. At the same moment, Ted left her side and approached the patron. At the bartender's insistence, the man blew into the mouthpiece of the plastic meter. As the reading showed too much alcohol in his bloodstream, he handed over his car keys.

"The cab'll be here in about five minutes." Ted informed him.

"Time for another drink?" the man asked, his smile beatific.

Ted poured a cup of coffee and set it on the counter. "On the house."

"Thanks, Ted," Lareana said as Trey re-entered the room. "You've taught me a lot."

"Any time."

"Can you stay for dinner?" Trey asked as they left the lounge. "We can get something quick. They rush the service for me when I ask."

"I'm really not hungry, and I've *got* to get home. Thank you, anyway."

"Okay, but you're missing out. I hear the food here is something to write home about." His easy smile invited an answering one. "I'll walk you to your car."

"Oh!" She turned back after unlocking the car door. "Are you going to be able to make the sentencing on Friday? It's at eleven."

"I'll be there," he reassured her. "If something comes up that I can't get out of, I'll let you know." He leaned on the door as she slid in and buckled her seat belt. "Call me when you get home?"

She nodded. "After I get Johnny down."

"Give him this for me." Trey kissed the tips of his fingers and laid them gently on Lareana's mouth. "Good night, Lareana, love."

The drive home was a kaleidoscope of sensations that left Lareana feeling more confused and worn out than before. She had a job that filled a life-long dream, but Trey was still asking her to accept the sale of liquor on the premises of the park.

But remember, the little voice from somewhere in her mind admonished, *you said you wouldn't force your views on anyone else. And he is doing all he can to keep drunk drivers off the roads. If more restaurateurs had his sensibility —*

Lareana rubbed her tired eyes. Spotting a fast-food place ahead, she turned off at the Fife exit and stopped for a cold diet drink. Back on the freeway, she at least felt more awake. But that didn't slow her internal dialogue.

And that's not all, another voice whispered. *You have fallen in love with someone who has been divorced. How are you going to work that out? I can just hear Aunt Sigrid now.*

Flashing red taillights from the screeching cars in front of her finally registered above the internal muddle. Lareana slammed on the brakes. Her car fishtailed and skidded, sliding to a stop with the front tires on the grassy median. She had no idea how she'd missed the car in front of her in the line of stopped vehicles.

"Thank you, God," she whispered as she waited for her heart to settle back into its customary position. She took a deep breath and pried her fingers from around the steering wheel.

After assuring the state patrolman she was all right, she pulled out to pass an accident. That had been too close a call.

When her doubts started nagging her again a few miles down the road, she deliberately turned on one of her tapes. She sang the rest of the way home. The problems weren't resolved, but she turned, safely, into the drive at last.

Even after her long phone conversation with Trey that night, Lareana didn't sleep well. Of course, Johnny's demanding an extra feeding in the middle of the night didn't help. Thoughts of Greaves continued to nag at her, along with the possibility of a saloon at Timber Country.

"If I didn't know better," she muttered as she turned her pillow over and thumped it into shape, "I'd think I was worrying. But since I have never been a worrier . . .

pictures of the creek in the evening come into my mind." Even that failed. Greaves was in the way.

Thursday didn't go much better. Lareana and Johnny trekked to the library for books, articles, any kind of information on drunk-driving laws. She came out with armloads of reading material.

When she got home, put Johnny down for a nap, and started reading, she couldn't concentrate. The material wasn't exactly inspiring, especially the statistics.

When she went to bed that night, she sadly decided that the best thing about the day was that it was over. Sadder still was the fact that this was a positive thought.

"You want to go in with me?" she asked Inga on the phone the next morning. "The sentencing shouldn't take long." *At least, I hope not.*

"If you need me, I will," Inga replied. "But today is my quilting day —"

"And you'd rather not miss it. That's okay. I'm taking Johnny, so I'll talk to you later." She finished getting ready and bundled the baby and all his trappings into the car. Trey had said he'd meet them at the courthouse.

More protesters had gathered outside the white building when they arrived, all of them carrying signs and parading back and forth. The chill wind hadn't seemed to dampen their spirits, but Lareana drew a blanket over Johnny's face to protect him from the cold, and hurried into the building. Her mother and father were waiting for her inside.

After hugging them both, Lareana asked, "Have you seen Trey yet?"

Margaret looked up from making grandma noises with Johnny. "No. Was he coming?"

Lareana nodded. She walked back to the doors and stared out the glass. The crowd had grown. She held the door open for Brian Campbell to wheel in his chair. Cathy Hanson followed him.

After greetings were exchanged, Brian unzipped his jacket and spread the opening wide. "How do you like my new T-shirt?" It was marigold with bold red letters across the chest spelling out — CORD.

"Hard to miss, that's for sure." Lareana smiled.

"Have you thought of joining?" Cathy asked. "We can always use more members. It would give you a chance to do something about people like Greaves. That's why I became a member."

Lareana was saved from answering as her

father called her to the courtroom. The proceedings were about to begin.

EIGHT

The judge entered.

Since their seats were in the back row, Lareana didn't see Greaves until everyone sat down. At the sight of his familiar slouch, all the anger she'd been shoving out of sight boiled up again. Her stomach clenched against the roiling. Her throat went dry.

She stared straight ahead until she felt a person take the seat next to her. At the same moment her concentration broke, Trey lifted her hand in his and squeezed. The sight of his face smiling encouragingly at her and the warmth of his body penetrated the coat of ice beginning to form around her power of reason.

The two lawyers who had been conferring with the judge took their places. The final act was about to commence.

"Will the defendant please rise?" the court clerk intoned.

Daniel Greaves pushed himself to his feet.

He pulled his shoulders erect and, with a visibly expelled breath, looked straight at the judge.

"Mr. Greaves, the bench finds that you have received an unprecedented number of driving-while-intoxicated citations. You have caused four accidents involving bodily injury to innocent people. Also you have been the recipient of every form of counseling and rehabilitation the state offers, all to no avail."

The judge looked over the rim of his glasses at the defendant. "Now you have been convicted of manslaughter in the death of John Amundson. I have no choice but to sentence you to no fewer than five and no more than ten years in the state penitentiary, sentence to begin immediately. Court dismissed." He banged the gavel.

The iron that had been holding Greaves upright melted. The man slumped in his chair, one hand over his eyes. A petite woman, tears streaming down her face, pushed open the swinging wooden gate and gathered him into her arms. A uniformed guard waited at his elbow.

Lareana felt no mercy. She didn't feel much of anything. Brian and Cathy gave her the victory sign when they caught her attention, but she couldn't respond.

Trey gathered her to him with one arm around her shoulders. He tried to turn her toward the exit, but she braced against his concern. Her attention remained riveted on the scene in the front of the room.

Greaves's lawyer shuffled his papers into his briefcase and, after a short conversation, clasped the man's shoulder and left.

The guard said something to Greaves. The convicted man replied, hugged the woman one more time, and just before he turned to go, raised his eyes to meet Lareana's. The unspoken request for forgiveness from this man who had been too proud to plead, met the inability of the woman to forget.

Daniel Greaves left the courtroom through a back door with two guards in attendance.

A soft voice at Lareana's side stopped her as she was about to leave the room. "Mrs. Amundson?"

Lareana turned. "Yes?"

"Daniel asked me to give you this," said the woman who had been hugging Greaves. She held out a plain white envelope. "And I want you to know how sorry I am . . . for the death of your husband." Her voice broke. "My Daniel . . . well, he's not a bad man, you know. It's just when he's been drinking —" Her pale eyes pleaded for understanding.

A cooling draught of compassion released some of the tension coiled in Lareana's body. She took a deep breath and patted the woman's hand which lay on Lareana's coat sleeve. "Thank you for speaking with me." Almost as an afterthought, she took the envelope from the unhappy woman and slipped it into her pocket.

Trey carried Johnny as they left the building. Most of the crowd had dispersed. Only a lone TV camera and crew remained.

"I don't know how I feel," Lareana responded to the questions. "I thought I would feel wonderful, glad that Greaves got what he deserved, but —" she looked directly into the camera's all-seeing eye — "it won't bring John back. And while I can rejoice that no one else will be injured because of that particular alcoholic driving the highways, what about all the others?"

"You'll be all right?" Margaret asked when they reached the cars.

"Yes, Mom. I'm fine. You go on home. I know you have all kinds of things to do." She hugged both her parents. "Thanks again for coming in."

"I'll call you Sunday with plans for Thanksgiving." Margaret spoke through her rolled-down window.

Swen stepped close to Lareana. "You're

not going to get involved with that CORD group, are you? Carrying signs and that kind of thing."

Lareana gazed pensively into his face. "I don't know, Dad. I just don't know. You've always told me to stand up for what I believe. Maybe this is the time I have to do that." She hugged him once again.

"I don't think he liked eating his own words," Trey whispered in her ear as the older couple drove off.

Lareana smiled. "No. They'd like to wrap their little girl in a down comforter and protect her, if they could." She shrugged. "But life isn't that easy, is it?"

That was one of those questions without an answer.

"Can I take you out to lunch, or would you rather I followed you home? We have to talk."

I'm not sure I want to talk, Lareana thought. *We might say things neither one of us is happy about.* She finished strapping Johnny's carrier in place. "I don't feel like going out to lunch." She shut the car door. "Guess I'll see you at the farm then."

Some reception, that, Trey thought as he followed her little car through the traffic and out to the country roads. A drizzle had started, graying the ageless hills and obscur-

191

ing the mountain.

When they arrived at Three Trees, Lareana set the baby's seat on the floor and automatically put the teakettle on. As she shrugged out of her coat, she heard a crackling in her pocket. Remembering, she pulled out the envelope. It looked like her mind felt right now — blank. She tossed it on the table.

When she returned from hanging up her coat, Trey held the letter, idly tapping it against one forefinger. "Don't you want to see what's in this?"

Lareana removed Johnny's bunting and lifted him to her shoulder. "I'm not sure." Holding the baby in one arm, she took mugs out of the cupboard with the other. "Coffee or tea?"

Trey watched for a moment as she tried to do three things with one hand. Then he went to her and removed Johnny from her arms. "At least let me do this for you." He sat down on one of the kitchen chairs and cuddled the baby on his lap, one arm tucked securely around Johnny's middle.

The baby gurgled and waved his fists, then aimed for the finger that had proved so tasty before. "Is he ever going to quit chewing?" Trey asked. "And slobbering?"

Lareana paused in her preparations and

watched the man and baby. They had taken to each other as if they'd known each other all the baby's short life, instead of for only a month. Had it really only been a month since she met him? It seemed like a lifetime, so much had happened. Only it wasn't just that —

"You will know," her mother had said years ago, "when you meet the right man, the man God intends for you to marry, to be happy with."

But, Mother, she thought, *John was that man. You felt it as much as I did. And what do I feel now?* Well, God said He would supply her needs. She should be grateful. *I will be, Father God. I promise I will.* She set their mugs on the table and slumped into the seat.

They sat in silence, sipping their tea. Trey played with the baby, and Lareana stared out the window. Even her chrysanthemums in the boxes lining the porch failed to color the gray afternoon. The clump of lilac had lost its leaves and reached bent fingers toward the lowering sky. Samson whined at the door.

"I'll go change," Lareana said when Johnny started to fuss. "He's getting hungry."

She returned in a plaid flannel shirt and

jeans. "I forgot to ask if you'd like some lunch." She finished tying her hair back with a Chinese-red scarf. "I can make you a sandwich."

Trey handed Johnny to his mother. "Why don't you feed him and I'll feed us? Just tell me where the fixings are." He walked into the living room, calling over his shoulder, "I'll just build this fire up first."

Lareana settled into her chair and drew the baby's quilt over her shoulder, cocooning Johnny in the warmth of her arm.

Trey left the stove door open, as he knew she liked, and returned to the kitchen. It was pleasant to hear him working around out there, frequently asking where things were and what she liked on her sandwich. Cupboard doors banged, the teakettle whistled, and Johnny nursed contentedly. When Samson whined again, Trey let him in with a pat and a friendly word.

"Do you want to eat in here or in the kitchen?" he asked, leaning one shoulder against the door jamb. He had removed his navy blazer which revealed a sweater vest the same blue as a lake under intermittent clouds. He'd rolled the sleeves of his white shirt up to the elbows and done away with the tie. Wool slacks matched the sweater, a grayed blue but with the promise of clear skies somewhere, sometime. "Hey, are you there?" Trey's smile brought her back to his question.

"Whatever." She returned his smile. "I can't make any major decisions today."

No, I bet not, Trey thought as he returned to his duties. *You look about done in.* Those shadows under her eyes appeared as if they'd been painted on with indelible ink.

On her way back from tucking Johnny into his crib, Lareana picked up the envelope from the table and brought it into the living room. Trey had arranged their lunch on the coffee table in front of the L-shaped, oatmeal-colored sectional. As she bit into the ham sandwich, she discovered just how hungry she was. Reaching for the envelope, she slit it open and began to read.

Dear Mrs. Amundson,
I know you will have a hard time believing this. I am aware of the animosity you feel toward me in the death of your husband, and I don't blame you. But I wanted to tell you how sorry I am. I know it doesn't do any good after the fact like this, but if sometime you can find it in your heart to forgive me . . .

Lareana found herself trying to read

through a veil of tears. She wiped them away with one hand and continued:

I can't even promise never to drink again, but I have been going to AA and haven't had a drink since the night of the accident. I can guess how I would feel in your place. God be with you.

Sincerely,
Daniel Greaves

Lareana's shoulders shook with the force of the sobs that wracked her body. She drew her knees up to her chest, curling into a ball of pain. The letter drifted to the floor.

At the first sign of her distress, Trey reached for her to take her in the shelter of his arms and comfort her, but her rigid form refused to yield. He watched her agony in silence, one hand stroking the back of her neck.

When the letter left her fingers, he picked it up and began to read. *Oh, my love.* His desire to bear her pain burned within his heart. *I had hoped this could be over by now but . . .*

Her weeping didn't lessen.

When his soothing hand didn't help, Trey turned and picked her up, cradling her in his lap whether she wanted it or not.

"I can't forgive him."

He could finally make some sense of her words.

"I've tried and I . . . I just can't." A fresh storm unleashed more incoherent ramblings.

Trey didn't try to decipher them. He just held her.

"Wh — what kind of person . . . what kind of Ch — Christian . . . am I that I can't forgive someone . . . when he asks?" She drew in a shuddering breath. "Today . . . when he looked at me, I — I knew what he wanted. J — Jesus says to l — love your enemies. *I can't do that.*" Her hands clenched and pounded on his chest. "I *can't.*"

Trey continued the murmurings she didn't seem to hear. It made him feel he was doing something, anything. He wiped the tears from her face and smoothed her hair back again and yet again.

He had no idea how much time had passed when the sobs turned into sniffles and the sniffles turned into the sleep of utter exhaustion. *Oh, my love. How can I help you?* His thoughts followed the rhythm of her breathing, periodically broken by a leftover sob.

Jesus, Trey prayed in the quiet of his mind as he held her, *only You can help her with this thing. I know You can because You helped me.*

Twilight had deepened to dark when Lareana awoke. She was huddled on the couch under a crocheted afghan. A friendly pool of lamplight drew her eyes to the man sitting in the rocking chair across from her. Trey had Johnny cuddled against his shoulder. With one minute thumb popped in his mouth and eyes half closed, the baby was enjoying the steady motion of the chair. Trey's eyes, at half-mast, held the same contented air.

Lareana's own eyes felt as if someone had thrown dust in them. Her throat was raw, and when she moved her head, an anvil took over, its beat pounding out the ebb and flow of her pulse. Her gaze turned to the letter lying open on the oak table.

She clenched her eyes against the sight of it, trying to wish away its existence. Before the letter, she could convince herself that Daniel Greaves didn't care, that he was beneath the human emotions of love and concern. No longer.

Father in Heaven, she prayed in the quiet of her mind, *I've come up against another one of the places that I can't, don't even want to, handle by myself. You know me. I've tried to do it . . . no . . . I'll be honest. I haven't tried* to forgive Daniel Greaves. *I was too angry. Now all I can ask is Your forgiveness and for You to forgive him. Thank You, Father.* Her quiet "Amen" definitely meant "so be it."

I'll just lie here and rest a moment, she thought. *Then I'll get up.*

Her moment stretched until the phone rang at nine-thirty. She heard Trey answer it. This time when she raised her head, the blacksmith had taken his anvil elsewhere. "Who was it?" she asked when Trey came back into the living room.

"Inga. She wondered how I made out feeding Johnny."

"Feeding Johnny?"

"Yes. You do that when a baby starts to cry." A warm smile deepened the creases around his mouth. "I called her and she told me where to find the bottled milk in the freezer. You really are efficient, you know." He sat down on the couch, pillowing her head in his lap. "I didn't know you could save breast milk like that."

"You learn all kinds of things on a dairy farm."

"As if that had anything to do with it." He stroked the hair back from her forehead.

"So where's Johnny now?" She wasn't sure if she wanted an answer or not. She hated the idea of moving.

"In bed."

"In bed?"

"Lareana, are you hard of hearing, or something? You keep repeating everything I say." A ghost of a proud chuckle over his accomplishments floated through his words.

"You know what I mean." She thumped him on the knee. "How did I sleep through all that?"

His stroking continued as he tried to sound offended. "We were *very* quiet. I explained to that young man in there that his mother had just had a very hard time and needed some rest. He agreed. And we were . . . quiet, that is."

"Just like that?"

"Well . . . sort of."

Quiet reigned again for a time.

"Thank you." Lareana knew she should get up and get going, but a pleasant lethargy had invaded her limbs. The warmth of Trey's thigh under her cheek, the gentle pressure of his fingertips blazing a line from her temple up into her hair, combined to keep her in her capsule of comfort.

"Trey?"

"Um-m-m?"

She pulled herself up to lean against his shoulder, her hair brushing his cheek. "I have something important to tell you."

His fingers stopped their soothing pattern. "Well?" His arm drew her closer, if that were possible.

"I love you." There it was out. A simple declarative statement. She raised her eyes to watch for expressions on his face.

"Are you sure?" It wasn't the response she'd expected.

"No. I go around telling that to strange men all the time."

Trey smothered his laugh in the sweet fragrance of her hair. "Oh, Lareana, my love. Just don't go finding any other men to say that to. This man's going to be all you can handle."

"Does that mean you love me?"

"Since the day I heard you messing up poetry for your cows. It was like a light went on in my life." He lowered his head so his lips were a hairsbreadth above hers. "And it's been getting brighter ever since." Their lips met and Lareana reached one arm around his neck. The kiss changed, from one of confirmation to one of growing passion.

Trey raised his head. "I think I'd better be on my way." He dropped a light kiss on the end of her nose. He repeated it after he had his coat on and was going out the door. "Good night, Lareana, love."

Lareana hugged herself with both arms as she trailed up the stairway to bed. She had barely crawled under the covers before sleep, a deep, restful sleep with no nightmares, claimed her.

That same air of peace and relaxation greeted her in the morning when Johnny's wake-up call informed her that mommies should feed babies — immediately. The peace stayed with her through her morning devotions. Now, when she prayed, her words seemed to go directly to the heart of God, not to ricochet off the ceiling. Daniel Greaves was not in the way anymore.

When she thought of Greaves, she no longer saw the arrogant defendant at the beginning of the trial. All she could see was a broken man crying in his wife's arms.

By the next morning, Lareana had succumbed to her inner prompting to write him a letter. That would bring the act of forgiveness full circle. It wasn't as hard as she had thought it would be. By the time she finished, she had written one to his wife, too.

I'm glad for you that Alcoholics Anonymous is helping. Rest assured that I forgive you and I know that if you ask,

God will, too —

In the following days, Lareana was to deal with the forgetting part of forgiveness. Pictures of Daniel Greaves leapt into her mind at the oddest times. Every time that happened, she replaced the pictures with one of Jesus. But just when she thought Greaves was vanquished from her mind's eye, he would reappear.

"I'm working at it, Mom," she said one day when she called Margaret. "I know I'm getting better because the anger's gone. It seems to come easier every day. When I remember Greaves, it doesn't hurt anymore."

"I'm glad," Margaret said. "People aren't made to live with hate and bitterness. They die from it . . . or maybe drink. Then, too, maybe this is God's way of reminding you to pray for Mr. Greaves."

Lareana felt her resentment flare up. "Mother!"

"I know you'll do the right thing." The pattern of her speech changed. "Now about Thanksgiving —"

Lareana was glad for the change in subject. They spent the next couple of minutes planning for the holiday. It was Lareana's turn to host this year, so dinner would be at

Three Trees. Margaret would take care of inviting the relatives. Thanksgiving was one of the few times during the year when all the aunts, uncles, and cousins got together. They usually fed about thirty people.

"I'm glad you feel up to it," Margaret said. "I was afraid there for a while —"

"I think I can do it now. During the trial I was so busy I had no time to think."

"Will Trey be there?"

"I hope so, but we haven't discussed holiday traditions yet." The silence lasted more than a moment. "He loves me, Mom."

"I know."

"And I love him."

"Yes."

"And you and Daddy approve?"

Margaret's sigh came from the depths of her mother heart. "We really like him, you know that. And we appreciate all he's done for you —"

"But?"

"Well, it's very soon after John's death."

"We've talked about that, Mom. I think John would approve of Trey."

"And Trey's selling liquor, Lareana. You know how the church feels about that, how we feel about it. We can't condone it."

"I know." Lareana sighed. "Give Dad a hug for me." She gently replaced the receiver.

In the next few weeks, Trey was so busy with meetings about Timber Country, Lareana felt she never saw him. Talking on the phone every day wasn't enough. One day she called her aunt who was a florist in Seattle and made a request.

When Trey arrived back at his office after a lengthy meeting with financiers for the theme park, he found a crystal vase filled with pink and fuschia bleeding hearts and lacy asparagus fern on his desk.

"My heart bleeds for you. Love, Lareana," the note read.

"Ditto." Trey said when she answered the phone. "Can you come up here? There's no way I can get away right now, except in the middle of the week."

"I know. And you need your sleep. If I came, how could you fit me into your schedule?"

"We'd at least have lunch together." He studied the calendar. "How about Tuesday?"

"Uncle Haakan and I are going to a farm dispersal sale that day. We're finally getting some new stock."

"Thursday?" The silence warned him he wouldn't like her answer.

"I have guests coming for lunch — Brian

205

Campbell and Cathy Hanson. They're bringing some people they think I should meet."

"CORD?"

"Yep."

"You're joining then?"

"I still haven't decided. That's what this meeting is all about. I've been reading reams of stuff on alcoholism, drunk driving, and the various programs and laws."

Trey's sigh could have been one of exasperation or defeat, Lareana wasn't sure which. She wasn't sure she wanted to know, either. "You'll be here for Thanksgiving, won't you?" she asked as the silence stretched between them.

"Of course I will. I get back from San Francisco on Wednesday evening. Can I bring anything?"

Lareana mentally reviewed the menu and who was bringing what. "Not that I can think of. Just yourself. And, Trey," she whispered before she hung up, "come as early as you can."

Lareana's meeting with the CORD group gave her plenty of fodder for thought. While Citizens Organized for Responsible Drinking seemed more fanatical than she wanted to be, she could see lots of good coming from their program. Mostly in public awareness.

They discussed the tough new laws in Oregon and the need for changes in Washington, too. All agreed that mandatory jail sentences would cut down on offenders. But as one of the legislators had said, "Where do you find the jail space?" There were certainly no easy answers.

One thing Lareana did agree to do. She would make herself available for television interviews. But she didn't promise to take Johnny every time, even though one person applied some pressure along that line.

In church on Sunday, Lareana wished Trey could be with her instead of in California. Having him with her in church was so special. There was something about God's order of things when a family worshiped together. There. She'd referred to themselves as a family again. How could anything that seemed so right be so wrong?

Pastor Jensguard probed a sensitive spot with his sermon topic. "Love your enemies . . . and pray for those who . . . persecute you," he read from the Bible in front of him.

"God has never called His people to the easy road," the pastor said. "Loving those who love you isn't hard, at least not usually." His smile encouraged the congregation to laugh at themselves a bit. "But praying for someone who has done you wrong . . . that's where God's grace comes in. He never expects us to grow by ourselves. But He does expect us to open ourselves to His channels of love and let that love pour through us."

Lareana would have liked to be able to shield her thoughts from God as well as she hid her feelings behind her "all is well" façade. *All right, so I'll pray for Daniel Greaves. I get the point. You don't have to hit me over the head with a two by four.* She smiled to herself.

"How's the heart, fair lady?" Trey's phone call late one evening was welcome, even if it was a poor substitute for the real thing.

"Still bleeding." Lareana cradled the phone against her ear and snuggled down in the blankets. "How's the dragon-slayer?"

"Lonely. Frantically busy. Beat. California may be sunny, but I haven't had time out of these offices to find out."

Lareana's heart went out to him at the weary timbre of his voice. "Oh, Trey. I wish there were something I could do for you."

"You could hop a plane."

"I meant right now, silly."

Their conversation extended over an hour. Nothing changed in their circumstances, but one more block was laid in the foundation of their growing love.

"Come home soon," she whispered as she laid the phone back in the cradle.

NINE

Lareana was out of bed before the birds on Thanksgiving morning.

Trey would be arriving today . . . but when? *I wonder what's early to him?* Her thoughts took off on flights of their own. She made her way downstairs to start the stuffing for the thirty-pound turkey she'd purchased.

Johnny heard her out in the kitchen and added his queries to her busy schedule.

"If you get such good response with a yell or two," Lareana muttered as she wiped her hands on the dishtowel, "what's going to happen when you can talk?"

When the baby caught sight of her, his happy grin joined flailing arms and jerking legs. His actions banished any twinge of annoyance. She hugged him close, then laid him on the changing table. By the time he was diapered and dressed again, Lareana could see the tinges of dawn cracking the cloud cover in the east. Grays turned to mauve, to violet and pink — joyful banners heralding a new day.

Johnny did not get a thrill out of the sunrise. He wanted to eat . . . now! And he told her so. Lareana sighed and turned from the opalescent dawn.

"One job finished," she breathed as she set up the playpen in the kitchen and settled him inside on his tummy with his favorite toys. She returned to the stuffing. Wrestling the huge bird into the sink so she could insert the stuffing reminded her of other Thanksgivings. John had always helped stuff the bird. The thought caused no pain, only a vague impression of sorrow, like looking into an ancient mirror. She shook her head at the realization. The healing she'd been praying for was progressing nicely.

She glanced at the clock and mentally calculated the time needed to bake the bird. Right on schedule. Without taking a break even for a cup of tea, she checked on Johnny in the playpen, added a few more toys, and flew back upstairs to get dressed.

Trey's coming. Trey's coming. Her thoughts beat time with her heart. She chose an amethyst wool shirtwaist dress out of the closet and threw it on the bed. Hers might have been the shortest shower on record.

She'd just finished clipping the sides of her hair up with mother-of-pearl combs and inserting amethyst studs in her ears when Samson activated his early warning system. A quick glance out the window confirmed her hopes. A familiar, silver Corvette was parked by the front gate.

The softly billowing skirt brushed the backs of her calves as she descended the stairs. She could hear Trey in the kitchen carrying on a conversation with a jabbering baby. They sounded perfectly content without her.

It may have sounded that way, but the look in Trey's eyes when she entered the kitchen dispelled any qualms she might have had.

Woman, you're definitely worth the wait, Trey thought when he saw her walk through the door. *I was afraid you were a figment of my imagination. Huh! If Seattle was too distant for us even to have lunch, California might as well have been the moon.* He rose from his kneeling position in front of Johnny, his eyes never leaving hers. When he opened his arms, she stepped into them.

"Ah, Lareana, love." He twined his fingers in her hair and raised her chin with the heels of his hands planted caressingly along her jawline. Kisses, lighter than the brush of hummingbird wings, closed each eyelid, cherished each dimple, and greeted her waiting lips.

"You smell like roses in springtime," he breathed when he drew back an infinitesimal distance. He brushed his lips back and forth across hers, igniting nerve endings wherever he touched. "And just in case you didn't suspect, I love you, I love you —"

"I love you." They shared the last declaration together, two minds, two hearts in unison.

They drew back, hands still locked around each other's waists as if afraid of letting go.

"I'm glad you define early like this." Lareana reached up to breathe a kiss into the cleft of his chin, something she'd dreamed of doing for quite some time. She rested her forehead against the thunder of his heart.

"Lareana."

"Um-m-m." She lifted her face to his, the smile she bestowed on him rivaling the dawn and causing his heart to constrict.

"I have something for you. But first I have to ask you something."

Lareana nodded.

"I wanted to do something spectacular. Maybe skywriting or fireworks. But I can't. I thought of sending it with a troop of clowns, but you mean too much to me."

His voice grew husky. "Maybe poetry would help, but I didn't want to wait long enough to compose a poem. Lareana, will you marry me?" His eyes searched hers for any sign of hesitancy.

Her simple "Of course" rang bells of joy through the corridors of his mind.

"You're sure?"

"This is a repeat of another conversation I remember. I don't go around accepting marriage proposals every day of the week." She threaded her fingers through the waves of hair on the sides of his head. "So you're just stuck with me," she said between kisses.

Johnny banged his chain of keys against the edge of the playpen.

"Or rather, with both of us."

"A package deal, huh? Something along the lines of love me, love my son?"

"And dog, cows, horses, and you have no idea how many relatives, many of whom will be here before we know it. Are you prepared to meet the troops?"

"I will be once you put this on." He drew a velvet box from deep in his pocket.

When he opened the lid, Lareana gasped with pleasure. The glinting diamond on an etched gold band was surrounded by chips of amethyst, cleverly designed to make both rings inseparable when locked together. He slipped the engagement ring of the pair on her ring finger, then raised her hand to his mouth and kissed the ring into place.

Lareana felt a tingling clear down to the tips of her toes. "Thank you," she whispered, wishing she could find words to tell him how she felt. "The ring's beautiful and . . . and so are you."

Marriage, she thought, *I'm . . . we're getting married. But when? Am I ready to remarry?* Her thoughts froze. *What will the family say?* She bit her lip. *Knowing them. . . . they'll have plenty to say.*

She held out her hand, letting the stones catch the light. The ring certainly did look lovely. "You have excellent taste."

"I know." He kissed the corner of her mouth. "I know."

Lareana laughed, a carefree sound that called up all the desires within him to protect her, to cherish her, to bring the song of laughter to her lips and help her share it with her world.

Johnny, tired of being ignored and ready for a bit of a snooze, interrupted their idyllic moment.

"Have you had breakfast yet?" Lareana asked after putting Johnny down. "I have cinnamon rolls in the freezer. They warm up quickly in the microwave."

"Sounds good. You'll eat with me?"

She nodded. "Then we'll set up the tables."

The living and dining rooms had become a banquet hall by the time they set up the three tables borrowed from the Grange hall. With orange candles and fall fruits and vegetables, Lareana created a centerpiece on each table. There wasn't a lot of room to move around, but everyone would have a place to sit.

"How many people are you expecting?" Trey eyed their labors dubiously. "It looks like you could accommodate an army."

"You'll think it *is* an army by the end of the day." Lareana clicked a tape into the stereo. Strains from *South Pacific* filled the air. "Not exactly a holiday piece, but it sure means a lot to me."

"What if we went there on our honeymoon?"

"Went where?" She laid out napkins.

"To the South Pacific. Spending February on warm, sunny beaches sounds like a bit of heaven to me."

Lareana stopped what she was doing. "Is that when you want to get married?"

"No. I'd like to marry you tomorrow or

216

next week at the latest, but February's the earliest I could get away for any kind of honeymoon. You know how much trouble we had getting together for lunch."

"We didn't make it."

"What'd I tell you?"

Lareana came around the table and, slipping her hands around his waist, leaned her cheek against his chest.

Turkey perfume greeted all the arriving guests after they'd been heralded by Samson. The house was soon full of laughing relatives, from young children who made a beeline for the haymow in the barn to elderly Aunt Karren who held court in the corner. The noise level rose accordingly, but it was a cheerful hubbub, a gathering of relatives who loved each other and showed it — most of the time.

"I've got something special to tell you," Lareana said, hugging both her parents when they entered the house. But someone interrupted with a question right then, and she got sidetracked. Lareana regretted that later.

Each group of relatives that arrived put more food on the tables. "Looks like we're feeding all the troops at Fort Lewis," Uncle Haakan said. That statement was his annual contribution to the festivities. Most of the time, he was an observer.

Trey met them all with a smile on his face and a special comment for each one of them. Within an hour they all felt they'd known him for years.

Lareana watched from the doorway as he sat with her Aunt Karren, listening to her tales of the trip from Norway. *Sure made her day,* Lareana mused as she watched the sparkle in the dimming eyes of her great-aunt.

"Where'd you find that hunk?" one of her cousins whispered. "He's a knockout."

"Would you believe in the milking parlor?" Lareana bit her lip to keep from laughing aloud at the expression on her cousin's face.

As the hot food was being transferred to the tables, Lareana sent one of the kids down to the barn to round up the others. When they were all assembled, Uncle Haakan asked the blessing.

Lareana had a hard time keeping her mind on the words his rich voice offered up. She was too full of her own thanks. And all of her gratitude had to do with the man standing beside her. Trey was not only filling in the gap left by John, he was already creating a place for himself. At the universal "Amen," everyone sat.

Lareana's ring went unnoticed until she joined everyone in passing platters and bowls heaped with food around the table. Her cousin, sitting directly across from her, nearly dropped the platter she was holding. "Lareana!" The astonishment in her voice effectively halted all conversation. "Is that an engagement ring on your hand?" All eyes stared at the flashing diamond on her finger.

Trey and Lareana exchanged a glance that said quite clearly, "well, the fat's in the fire now." Together they stood. Lareana nodded at Trey.

"This morning I asked Lareana to marry me and she accepted." His voice carried to every ear in the room, even to half-deaf Aunt Karren.

"But she hardly knows him," the old woman's querulous voice responded. "And John's only been gone a few months."

The silence was brief but spoke volumes. Uncle Haakan rose to the occasion. "Congratulations, Lareana. Trey, welcome to the family." The buzz of conversation resumed, but the announcement was not mentioned again.

I was afraid of this, Lareana thought. *Guess I know this bunch pretty well after all. I should have warned Trey.* She peeped sideways at his handsome profile. *And it'll probably get worse before it gets better.*

If the groans and moans from around the tables meant anything, dinner was a huge success. When the men exited to the sofas and chairs, the women began clearing the table. Trey didn't join the men. He pitched in with willing hands, carting dishes and food back to the kitchen.

Once he overheard two women whispering, "How long has John been dead now? Only a few months, isn't it?" asked the first. "Yes, and this man's been divorced, too, you know," replied the second. "How can Margaret bear that?"

It's not Margaret's problem, Trey wanted to say. *It's mine and Lareana's and we don't consider it a problem. Why should you?* But he knew the answer. These older people had lived with such dictates for a long time.

Lareana heard the whispers, too. And caught the speculative glances cast her way. One aunt took her aside.

"Lareana," she said, her eyes stern above an equally serious mouth. "You know the saying, 'Marry in haste; repent at leisure.' I can't bear to think of you rushing into marriage with that man, no matter how charming he is." She shook her graying head. "Can't you at least wait awhile?"

Johnny whimpered. *Saved by the bawl,*

Lareana punned as she excused herself to retrieve her crying son. *The old bat. Who does she think she is?* Another voice answered the first. *Your Aunt Sigrid, that's who.* It was like a debate going on in her head. Aunt Sigrid had always been one of her favorite people.

"But she doesn't mind telling me what she thinks." Lareana closed the debate as she changed Johnny's diaper in the quiet of his room. She settled herself in a rocker by his crib and let him enjoy his Thanksgiving dinner.

Her thoughts winged upward. *Lord, I know what I want to do here and I believe You sent Trey to me. You talk about love and forgiveness. That's what You've made me learn. Forgiveness.* A smile smoothed the worry lines from her forehead. She nodded. *Thanks.*

When she reentered the living room, she felt a definite coolness in the air. While dusk was falling, no one but Uncle Haakan had made any move to leave.

She drew her mother out into the kitchen. "I wanted you and Dad to be the first to hear about our engagement," she said. "That's what I was referring to when you got here. I know how you feel, but —"

"Lareana —" Margaret put her arms

around her daughter — "you know we love you, no matter what. We're afraid you're taking on some tremendous problems, but our love for you comes first."

"Thanks." Lareana hugged her back. "I know that, but it always helps to hear it." She took her mother by the arm. "Now, please back me up while I stand up for what I believe, okay?"

Lareana assumed a relaxed pose in the middle of the area where the adults had congregated. For once, it wasn't women in the kitchen and men in the living room. "I have something I'd like to say to all of you." She glanced from person to person, catching her relatives' attention.

Trey watched from the sidelines, proud of her spirit, but unsure what she planned to do.

"You all stood 'round me when John was killed. Some of you stayed with me." She smiled at her Aunt Karren. "Others came and helped with the chores, even the haying when Uncle Haakan and I needed you." Several of the men nodded. "You have called me when I was in the dumps and helped me with the canning when Johnny and I first came home. You're a wonderful family, and I feel proud to be part of you."

She glanced at Trey long enough to get an

approving nod. "But I have learned something in the last few months that I'd like to share with you. With Trey's help, I had to learn to forgive the man who killed my husband. Aren't we all given chances to begin again? I believe this is our chance, mine and Trey's, and I don't think time or the past should stand in our way. Anytime is always the right time for love." She paused, her eyes going to the mantel where a picture of John was displayed. "And I know we have John's blessing." No one moved. No one said a word. Lareana found her mother's eyes swimming in tears, and her father dropped his head.

Trey swallowed hard to dislodge the lump her words brought to his throat. *With a woman like that in my corner, how can I lose? Thank you, Father, for this second chance.*

Lareana moved to his side. "There's fresh coffee in the kitchen if any of you would like some. And plenty of leftover pie."

It was as if her words released the spell that had held them all motionless. Some stood and stretched. Others started visiting with the people next to them. Aunt Inga came over to where Trey and Lareana were standing.

"Now don't you worry." Her chirpy voice radiated good will. "They'll come around.

223

You just wait and see. And, Lareana, I agree with you wholeheartedly. Welcome to the family, Trey."

The evening sped by as some left and others refilled their coffee cups. Lareana's parents had to go home but shared hugs with both Lareana and Trey as they left. Johnny woke up again, delighted with all the opportunities to entertain.

"That's one of the friendliest babies I've ever seen," Inga remarked. "He almost never cries."

"If I didn't know how prejudiced you are, I'd think you were the proud grandma," Trey teased her gently.

"Couldn't love him more if I were." She tapped Trey's arm with a gnarled finger. "There's an extra bed at our house tonight if you'd like. Save you a long drive."

"Thank you. I accept." Trey felt warmth and approval in Inga's display of hospitality.

Even Aunt Sigrid hugged the pair of them before she left.

"Please listen to the love in your heart," Lareana whispered in her aunt's ear during the embrace, "and accept him."

"I'll try, child. But I just don't know." The elderly woman shook her head as she walked down the steps.

"What a day." Lareana collapsed on the

sofa after the last guest had departed. She kicked off her shoes and leaned against the backrest, yawning and stretching.

Trey resisted the urge to join her until she lifted the drift of golden hair from her neck with both hands and let it fall. He gave in, the lure of gold too great.

"Enticing is against the rules if you want me to make it to Inga's house tonight," he murmured against the sweetness of her lips.

"My, how you talk, sir." Her eyebrow arched, reminiscent of bygone days when women hid behind fans. "But then, talk is cheap. Or so they say."

"Then let's stop talking if you rate it so poorly."

"And — ?"

"Do this instead." His lips took the place of his words. The kiss was worth the wait.

If Trey and Lareana thought they'd been busy before Thanksgiving, they were in shock afterwards. They discovered again, much to their dismay, that the distance between Seattle and Yelm didn't lend itself to easy commuting, especially since they were both going ninety miles an hour in different directions.

Lareana awoke the first Saturday in December to two inches of snow creating a fairyland outside her windows. By the time she called Trey and invited him to go with them to cut the Christmas tree, it was twice as deep.

Just before he arrived, the sun came out, painting the world in diamond glitter on fluffy ermine. Lareana had Johnny all ready in his backpack. She handed Trey the saw and shrugged into the straps of the pack.

"I'll take the kid, you get the tree. Even trade." Her smile rivaled the icicles on the trees for brightness.

"Which way?" Trey took her mittened hand in his. He held the handsaw up toward the sun, studying the pointed edges. "This doesn't look sharp enough to cut pussy willows."

"Well, since pussy willows won't be out for a time, you can practice on a pine tree and develop your muscles."

He studied the saw again. "Maybe it'll cut butter, softened that is."

"Gripe, gripe, gripe." She shifted the backpack. Johnny kept bouncing and kicking every time Samson ran by, frolicking in the snow.

Choosing the tree was not an easy task. Lareana had to look at every one, at least once. As they meandered back and forth through the woods, Lareana and Trey kept up a steady discussion of Timber Country, farming, CORD, and their wedding date. The last topic occupied most of the conversation.

When Lareana finally decided on the perfect tree, Trey sawed it down and hoisted it to his shoulder . . . for a distance of at least a hundred feet. Then moved by common sense and a complaining back, he dragged it the rest of the way.

"Did you have to pick out the biggest one?" he puffed as he maneuvered the tree through the barbed wire fence. "Where are you going to put such a monster?"

"You'll see," was her pert reply — just before she pelted him with a snowball.

"You'll get yours, when you don't have that guardian on your back."

The tree did fit right in the stairwell as she'd planned. And it was a beauty, full and permeating the house with pine perfume.

"My 4-H club is coming tomorrow to decorate it." Lareana stared at the boxes of decorations she and Trey carted down from the attic. "That'll be the first of my entertaining for the season. I love it."

"What other parties are you planning?"

"CORD and the Homemakers Club." She thought for a moment. "And the Dairy Wives."

"Would you like to hostess a party for me?"

"Are you serious?"

"Of course. Ada will do all the preparations. You just bring your natural graciousness to make everyone feel at home. Since you do that without trying, it should be a fun evening."

"I'd love to." She snuggled under his arm. "When?"

When became the operative word. The days ran by like sprinters going for the gold.

Lareana had her first taste of distress when the women from her Homemakers Club brought a bottle of brandy to put in the eggnog. That had been the custom in the past and Lareana had forgotten to inform them any differently.

Then on the night of the CORD gathering, someone brought homemade batter and rum for hot buttered rum. When Lareana questioned it, they looked at her as though she'd lost her senses.

Cathy took her aside. "We don't say that people can't drink. You know that, Lareana. We try to help them learn to drink with moderation . . . responsibly."

Lareana swallowed back her retort and got out the Christmas mugs. She and John had bought them for parties just like this . . . for hot buttered rum, as a matter of fact.

But resentment over her inability to stay with her decision of no liquor in her house nagged at her. She could have kicked them all out. Or tossed the alcohol out the back window. But where did her rights end and theirs begin? Surely she should be able to make the choices in her own home.

It seemed everywhere she went, people were offering "holiday cheer." Had it always been this way? She thought back. Yes, it had. *I just didn't notice because I like eggnog and hot buttered rum, too.* There, the admission was out. Now what?

Trying to keep her life in balance and remember the real reason for Christmas seemed harder as the day approached. She still hadn't decided on a gift for Trey. All her other gifts were either made or bought, already wrapped, and placed under the tree.

Johnny thought the Christmas tree enchanting. He sat for hours watching the flickering lights and brightly colored ornaments.

Next year, Lareana thought, *we'll probably have to put the tree in the playpen. Or hang it from the ceiling.*

Trey watched her frantic pace with concern. He wasn't too excited over her continued frustration with the serving of alcoholic beverages, either. Every time they talked about Timber Country, somehow the subject gravitated back to the saloon.

"I'm tired of talking about it!" he flared up one night. "Can't we leave it alone for a while? It's still a long time until the place opens."

"But the architects are designing it now. I just don't see how I can support a place that serves alcoholic drinks, much less help plan it." She scrubbed a tired hand across her forehead, much like a weary child. The blue circles had reappeared under her eyes.

"Lareana —" His voice flicked like the tip of a bullwhip. "Let's drop it." He rammed his hands into the back pockets of his jeans and went to stand in front of the window. The twinkling lights draped around the porch roof cast shadows of blue and red across his face.

He turned to her, remorse written like a banner across his face. "I'm sorry. I'm just too tired to argue, and so are you. And besides, I love you too much ever to want to fight with you." He walked back to her and drew her into his arms. "It'll work out, love, somehow. I promise."

I don't know. Lareana tried to keep the doubt out of her mind. At that point, it didn't seem possible.

TEN

It didn't get any better.

The day of Trey's party, Lareana wanted to call in sick. She'd spent the morning taping a town hall style discussion for a television program to be aired between Christmas and New Year's. A heckler in the studio audience had managed to get in a few slurring remarks like "self-righteous prohibitionists" and "do-gooders" before he was hustled out. While the knowledge that starting the tape over was supposed to make her feel better, it didn't help a whole lot. The producer tried to reassure her after the taping. The program looked good and would be very effective, or so he said.

She still hadn't found that perfect present for Trey, and Christmas was only a week away.

She left for Seattle early and, on an uncharacteristic whim, stopped at an arts and crafts fair at the Tacoma Mall. The covered mall was packed, both in the many stores and the wide decorated aisles. Tinny Christmas carols tinkled faintly through the hubbub of harried shoppers.

The perfect gift, displayed on a navy velvet cloth, appeared to be waiting just for her. The artist cast his work in bronze and had many pieces on display, but Lareana failed to notice his other wares. *The gift* stood out.

The bronze depicted an early logging scene. The burly lumberjack, a perfect replica down to his suspenders, knit stocking cap, and an ax handle across his shoulder, stood watching a giant fir tree in its death plunge.

Lareana could hear the cry of "Timber!", the shattering of branches. She could smell the pungent scent of fresh fir and sense the logger's satisfaction.

The artist waited patiently on the other side of the U-shaped table. "You like that one."

Lareana raised her eyes to encounter the far-seeing gaze of an outdoorsman. He might have doubled as the model for the piece. "Yes. It's just the thing." She pulled out her checkbook. "Are you, by chance, a logger?" she asked as she wrote. "You create such vivid images." She touched the screaming branches forever captured in midfall.

"Have been." His answer, though short, was not abrupt, but demonstrated an economy of words.

Lareana studied several other pieces. "And a fisherman . . . and a farmer?"

The man smiled, the kind of smile that deepened the weathered creases around his mouth and crinkled the crow's-feet at his eagle-keen eyes, a smile that invited her response. "Whatever's at hand."

Lareana nodded, her smile deepening in imitation of his. All the while her fingers were busy exploring, comforting the dying fir tree.

"I'll be getting in touch with you," she said, as she finished writing her check and slipping his business card in her billfold. "I know just the showcase for your work." *Maybe,* she thought after wishing him a Merry Christmas, *he'd like to cast his scenes right there at the park.*

While the bronze was no more than eight inches tall, it was heavy enough that Lareana was glad she'd found a parking place up close. All in all, the excursion had only taken twenty minutes. She would arrive for the party early.

Trey had given her good instructions, so she was able to drive right to the underground parking garage of his condominium.

Lareana unhooked her garment bag from the back hanger and picked up her carryall. Though thoughts of a country mouse arriving in the big city played in the back of her mind, she conveyed an air of poise and assurance. She alone knew it was fake.

Trey hadn't told her that the tenth floor was the penthouse. He hadn't warned her of ankle-deep carpeting in the hall or carved double wooden doors at the entry. This country mouse wanted to turn tail and run.

Lareana pushed the buzzer.

Ada fit her name. When the housekeeper answered the door, she took one look at the lovely young woman standing in the hall and beamed a welcome that would have melted a heart of concrete.

"My stars!" She held the door wider. "If you aren't everything Mister Trey has been raving about. Come in. Come in." She shut the door again and took Lareana's hand. "My dear, I'm so happy to meet you." Lareana felt she'd just been made part of the family.

"Mr. Trey said for you to make yourself ready. He'll be here a bit later." Ada led her charge down a hall to a bedroom decorated in royal blue. The bathroom matched, with dark blue fittings and thirsty blue towels.

"I'll hang up your things, and you take a

bath or whatever you like. If you're hungry, I'll bring you a tray." Ada stopped chattering to repeat, "I'm so glad you're here."

Lareana was too, as she slipped into the tub redolent with rose-scented, bubbling bath oil and settled her head against a foam neckrest. With her hair pinned on top of her head, she let herself relax for the first time in days.

She had finally managed to tear herself away from the luxury of the Jacuzzi tub and was standing in front of the bedroom mirror, nearly ready, when Trey knocked at her door. "Come in," she said as she clipped on a dangling crystal earring.

Lareana turned for his inspection, glittering in an ice-blue satin, floor-length gown. It fell freely from slight gathers at her shoulders, grazing her hips and swishing as she floated across the floor and into his arms. The modest, draped neckline seemed to draw attention to sparkling dangles in her ears.

Trey finally brought his lips to hers, ending the ache of abstinence and calling into being the joy of reunion.

"I think we have to go, my lady," he whispered in her ear, his breath sending tremors of delight rampaging through her system.

I'd rather stay right here. Lareana leaned closer rather than breaking the contact. *Let them have their party without us.*

Trey dropped a last kiss on her forehead. He began humming, softly, only for her ear . . . "Some Enchanted Evening."

Lareana ordered her internal aerial exhibitionists back to the wings. *I feel more like "We're Off To See The Wizard . . ."*

To Lareana, the living room seemed about an acre in size. The decorations were magnificent, a striking advertisement for the florist who had created the scene. A flocked tree, resplendent in shimmery gold and cut-glass ornaments, glistened against the black of a wall-long window. Fat white candles, surrounded by flocked greens and golden balls, graced the mantel of a white marble fireplace and marched down the laden dining table. The caterers, too, had done their job well.

The holiday decorations matched the sophisticated decor of the steel-gray room with black and white accents. *One would never know the real Trey by studying the place where he lived,* Lareana thought.

By the end of the evening, she felt that way about his guests, too. Polite and pointless conversations had never held any enjoyment for her. She smiled in all the right places, and repeated all the right words, but deep inside she felt someone screaming to be let out.

Is this what my life's going to be like? Lareana thought, leaning her back against the coolness of the fireplace. Trey ran a multimillion-dollar business, and these people were his friends and associates. She grimaced inwardly at the shrieking laughter of a svelte woman in a deep-cut, black dress. But the eternal smile Lareana had ordered never left her face.

How could I meet them again on a business day and not remember what fools they made of themselves tonight? Is it all because of the liquor? Or is that just a convenient excuse?

"Down the hall and to the right," she answered the question without a break in her inner monologue. *Lord, I don't want any part of this . . . this circus. But I love Trey and I want to marry him. And entertaining is important to his business.*

Lareana played the perfect hostess. The role became her, but it remained a role, at least for this audience. She even had Trey fooled until he took a moment to refill her glass of sparkling water and brush a kiss across her icy lips.

"Are you all right?" He handed back her glass.

She nodded, not trusting herself to speak.

"That's my lady fair." But he gave her a questioning glance before he turned to a guest requesting his attention.

It took all her grace and humor to put off the overtures of one slightly balding banker. She did it without even offending him. She heard him expounding her virtues as a conversationalist a bit later.

As the hour grew late and the drinks flowed more freely, the din assaulted Lareana's ears until she could no longer bear the tumult. She returned to the lovely room where she'd dressed and retrieved her coat from the walk-in closet. Shrugging her arms into the sleeves, she crossed to the sliding glass doors and let herself out onto the rooftop garden overlooking Shilshol Bay. She ambled over to the half-wall and leaned her elbows on the railing.

But even out there she couldn't get away from the party.

"So you couldn't stand it anymore, either." A slurry voice announced the man who spoke at her side.

"Oh! You startled me." She turned to find the architect who'd been the chief proponent of the saloon at Timber Country.

"You're beautiful." He stepped from the shadows enough to peer at her with bleary eyes. "That Trey is one lucky fellow."

Lareana murmured a "thank you" but couldn't think of anything else to say. She needn't have bothered.

Charlie — he'd introduced himself — did all the talking. "I don't usually drink like this, you know. It's all her fault."

Lareana was afraid to ask who, but she succumbed to politeness . . . and curiosity.

"My wife. She left me. Took our kids, the dog, and the best car. Says I'm married to my job." He shook his head. "Can you beat that? All these years I've been supporting her, working my tail off for her and the kids." Sniffs accompanied his tale. He rested his forehead on his clasped hands on the railing. "That house is so empty, I hate to go home."

Lareana felt tears welling up in her throat at the man's confession.

"And so I drink. It takes away the pain."

Until tomorrow, Lareana wanted to tell him, *until you wake up again.*

"D'you ever need to get drunk?" His question caught her by surprise.

"No," she responded simply, "I try to let God take care of my troubles. Works better that way."

A long pause broken only by the hoot of a departing freighter gave her time to wish for more brilliant words.

"Good night, Lareana." He touched a limp hand to his forehead. "I need another drink." He stumbled back toward the brightly lighted room.

Lareana shivered in the brisk breeze blowing off the sound. She pulled her coat tighter around her. *Lord,* she continued the prayer she'd started earlier, *isn't serving alcohol to someone like that aiding and abetting? Doesn't that make Trey just as guilty? What am I going to do?* She stared out at the pinpoint lights of the town of Winslow and its ferry terminal on the tip of Bainbridge Island. The dark waters in between seemed like the chasm dividing her lifestyle from Trey's.

She was about to go in when she overheard Charlie muttering his goodbyes.

Trey answered with a question. "Where are your car keys, my friend?"

Charlie had grown obnoxious. His answer made Lareana's ears burn.

"I don't care," Trey responded. "No one leaves my parties drunk and drives home. I've already called a cab for you. The fare's on me. Just give me your car keys. One of my men will deliver your car tomorrow."

Charlie's expletives were becoming more creative.

"It won't do you any good. The doorman will only put you in a cab. My orders." The two moved out of earshot.

"Thank you." Lareana whispered the words against Trey's lips as he kissed her goodbye in the garage later.

"For what?"

"Oh, for living up to what you say." She planted another offering in the region of his cleft chin and snuggled closer.

"I wish you'd stay." He tipped her face up with one finger. "I hate to see you driving at night."

"I know." She got in her car and closed the door. Rolling down the window, she asked with a smile, "Would you call a cab for me, too?"

Lareana sang along with the stereo the afternoon of Christmas Eve. She played the carols over and over, never tiring of either the music or the message. She checked the time . . . again. Trey had said he'd come early. One of these days she'd learn to set times for things. To her, "early" was like Thanksgiving morning. What a nice "early."

She stopped wiping the counter. "What child is this who laid to rest . . . ?" *How I love that baby of mine,* she thought. *Mary must have felt the same way.*

Samson's barking jerked her back to the present. She checked the window. Sure enough, her biggest Christmas present had arrived. She met Trey at the door, her long red skirt aswirl and her lips promising love for the ages.

"Merry Christmas!" He hugged her, his arms wrapped around her as if she might disappear in a puff of smoke. "You smell of —" he buried his nose in her hair — "roses and spice and . . . you." He set her back on her feet. "This has been a mighty long week. Let's not have too many more of these."

"Meaning you want to tie the knot —"

"Or jump over the broom —"

"Would a vacuum cleaner work?" She batted her eyes at him. "I'm a modern woman . . . no brooms."

He swept her up again. "Woman, today we set a date."

Lareana didn't argue.

"I have something for you," he said as she took his coat. "Do you want to open it now or later?"

"Silly man. You should never offer me a choice like that. My mother always made us wait until after Christmas Eve services." She drew him into the living room. The packages under the tree covered up the lower branches, a colorful pile that spoke of love and devotion.

"Good grief." Trey stared at her in dismay. "Are *all* your relatives coming tonight?"

"No, just us."

"Then who are all those presents for?" She laughed up at him. "Old family custom. Deliver all packages on Christmas Day. That way no time for hanky-panky."

Johnny's summons interrupted their tryst under the mistletoe. "Let's go get him and open our presents now," Trey whispered in her ear.

Lareana leaned back, pretend shock written on her face. She giggled. "I won't tell if you won't. But just the ones from each other."

Johnny had more fun with the paper than with the cuddly pink pig that was his gift from Trey. But when his mother took the paper away, he found the pig's ear equally satisfying — in his mouth, of course. Trey and Lareana left him to his chewing and proceeded with their own presents.

Trey didn't say a word when he opened the package containing the bronze. He couldn't. He leaned over and touched her lips with his, his gratitude implicit in the caress.

"The business card is in the box, too," she said between kisses. "The man's a natural for Timber Country."

Trey placed a large box on her lap. "Your turn."

Lareana picked it up and shook it. "Light and no noise. You're trying to make me think something is in here. Right?"

Trey nodded. "Just open it."

The first thing she found, after tearing the red foil wrapping aside and lifting the lid, was an envelope. The card inside read: "No liquor will be served in Swen's Cookshack. Timber Country Saloon will specialize in sparkling cider, root beer, sarsaparilla, and other soft drinks — served in icy mugs, of course, as befits a saloon."

Trey held her in his arms until her tears dried. "That's supposed to make you happy." He stroked her shoulder with a loving hand.

"I . . . it d — does. I always cry when I'm happy." She wiped her cheeks with her fingertips. Eyes still shimmering, she stared for a moment deep into Trey's soul. "Why?" she asked softly, her hands covering his. "What made you change your mind?"

"I've been changing and unchanging my mind, so I've had long talks with many of the family amusement park owners from across the country. The general consensus is, no liquor in the parks. The ones that have it serve only beer and wine, and in very restricted situations. So I went against the recommendations of my designers and —"

"And I love you, Mr. Timber Country." Lareana threw both her arms around his neck and nestled her lips just beneath his ear. The box flew to the floor in her enthusiasm.

Before his mind was totally absorbed, Trey picked up the box and set it back in her lap. "There's more."

She dug further in the box. Another envelope. This one contained two tickets to Tahiti for February fifteenth.

"Do you think we can make it? The three of us?" Trey wiped her tears away this time, and his own eyes had a suspicious shine.

"Um-hmm." The stars in her eyes rivaled the ones in the heavens. "I can't think of a better way to celebrate Valentine's Day than with a wedding, especially when it's ours."

After Johnny interrupted their embrace this time, they took turns wiping each other's eyes. The baby ignored them, however, when Samson joined him on the floor in front of the sofa. All that long, golden dog hair was too good an opportunity to miss, and his baby fingers took advantage of the situation. Samson sighed, his fine head between his paws.

Trey kissed his wife-to-be once again, on the tip of her nose. "There's more."

Lareana shuffled tissue paper around until she found a tiny box way down in the corner. It was oblong and velvet, covered in deepest blue. The three sapphires inside winked in the glow of the tree lights, one on a fine gold chain and the other two mounted on gold studs for her ears.

"I've always thought these would match your eyes," he said as he latched the chain around her neck. "And now I know." He turned her face with the tip of his finger, so the jewels twinkled again. "They do." He breathed kisses where each sapphire rested, then trailed matching caresses over her jawline, covering her mouth with his, warming her with the strength of his caring.

Lareana felt herself soar with the clouds, searching the far reaches of the heavens but always remaining in the unbroken circle of Trey's love.

Later, shoulder to shoulder with Trey in the candlelit church sanctuary, Johnny sound asleep in her arms, Lareana listened to the old, old story with a special joy in her heart. Her life had certainly changed since last year at this time. The songs flowed around her. "It Came Upon a Midnight Clear" . . . a different enchanted evening.

EPILOGUE

T-i-m-b-e-r-r-r!

Lareana flinched as the fir tree crashed to the ground. With a rattle, the huge chain barring the front gate dropped to the ground. Three plaid-shirted men with suspenders that hiked logging pants above cork boots stood ready. One with a wash tub and thumping stick, one with a kazoo, and the last with a tin horn; they would lead the proper band. Proper, that is, with instruments, but with costumes as individual as the loggers themselves.

The band burst into a toe-tapping rendition of "Oh, Susanna," the parade began, and Timber Country, Trey's dream brought to reality, was officially open to the public.

Riding in the gilded wagon behind the huge gray Percherons and waving to the crowds lining the street was easy. Keeping Johnny from climbing up to the driver's seat and corralling Trish in her lap at the same time was *not* easy. In fact, it was downright impossible. Lareana was already feeling more than a bit warm. A trickle of perspiration joined other drops down her spine. How did those women of early years manage?

When Trey swung aboard, she breathed a sigh of relief. Tricia waved her arms and chortled her approval at the handsomely bedecked man across from her.

He doffed his beaver top hat at her and checked the time from a golden pocket watch complete with looped chain.

"Right on the minute." He grinned at his wife, equally resplendent in a washed silk dress of royal blue. She had a hard time keeping her black lace-trimmed matching parasol upright. Trish loved the handle . . . in her mouth.

Trey's jacket and Lareana's dress matched in hue if not in fabric. Johnny and Trish, miniatures of their parents, ignored the period costumes. The sights were more fun.

"Here, let me take her," Trey said, gathering the squirming infant into his arms. At seven months, Trish didn't always want to be gathered. She wanted to get to wherever the action was . . . preferably under her own power.

Lareana breathed a sigh of relief. She

straightened herself and her skirts and turned her attention to the park. A group from CORD waved their banners and cheered as the wagon passed. Lareana waved back, proud of her work in the organization and the changes they were promoting.

The aroma of freshly baked apple pizza was already drawing crowds to the chuck wagons like kids to an ice cream vendor. One of the men from the Grange raised his slice of pizza in salute.

As the wagon passed the log ride, she could hear riders screaming their delight. She shivered as she remembered their trial run. The drop into the millpond would thrill the most adventurous.

Next to the blacksmith shop, the creator of Trey's bronze logging scene was patiently explaining the process of his art to spectators as he designed another piece. He waved to Lareana as the wagon passed by.

After wending their way through the entire park, the wagon delivered them to the front door of Swen's Cookshack. As they stepped onto the wooden porch steps, Lareana glanced up at her husband. Behind him a sign boasted the old-time delicacies to be enjoyed within. She remembered all the hours, the successes and failures of experimenting with recipes to fill that menu. Even Aunt Sigrid had finally pitched in.

Trey circled Lareana's waist with one arm, trying to hold Trish with the other. He managed it, even when she stuck one baby finger in between his teeth. Her deep belly laugh was the kind that demanded everyone join in. And everyone did. All the relatives gathered on the porch chuckled together, even Uncle Haakan couldn't resist.

Lareana glanced up at the sign, *Swen's Cookshack,* and then at her mother and father. The pride in their eyes caused tears to blur the scene for her.

Thank you, Father, for this day and all the people around us, she prayed silently. *And for the dream you gave Trey to bring happiness to so many people.*

She reached up and planted a kiss on the corner of Trey's mouth and another on the baby's fair cheek. She leaned over to drop a third on Johnny's forehead.

"Hoorah for Timber Country!" She echoed the cheers of the crowd as Johnny, holding monstrous scissors guided by his grandfather Swen's hands, cut the ribbon across the door.

"That's some boy, that son of ours." To be heard above the cheering, Trey spoke directly into her ear.

251

Lareana turned her head just enough to brush a fleeting kiss across his lips. "Takes after his dad."

The joy in Trey's eyes promised years of laughter and new dreams to build.

ABOUT THE AUTHOR

Lauraine Snelling is a full-time writer who has several books published, including the popular Golden Filly Series for junior-high girls. *Song of Laughter* won the Golden Heart award for excellence in fictional romance.